BOOKED
FOR
A
HANGING
▼

Also by Bill Crider

BOOKED
FOR
A
HANGING

BILL CRIDER

ST. MARTINS PRESS
NEW YORK

Design by Tanya M. Pérez

Library of Congress Cataloging-in-Publication Data

Crider, Bill
    Booked for a hanging / Bill Crider.
        p.   cm.
    "A Thomas Dunne book."
    ISBN 0-312-08149-9
    I. Title.
    PS3553.R497B66   1992
    813'.54—dc20   92-24913
                                                                         CIP

First Edition: October 1992

10 9 8 7 6 5 4 3 2 1

THIS BOOK IS RESPECTFULLY DEDICTATED
TO THE MEMORY
OF ANTHONY BOUCHER,
WHOSE "CRIMINALS AT LARGE" COLUMNS
IN THE NEW YORK TIMES BOOK REVIEW
REMAIN THE BEST UNCOLLECTED GUIDE TO MYSTERY READING
IN EXISTENCE

AND

TO LEN AND JUNE MOFFATT
AND THEIR GRAND CO-CONSPIRATORS,
WITHOUT WHOSE CONNIVANCE
THE BOUCHERCON,
THAT WONDERFUL ANNUAL MEETING OF MYSTERY FANS
FROM ALL OVER THE WORLD,
WOULD NEVER HAVE BECOME REALITY

SHERIFF DAN RHODES STARED AT THE COMPUTER MONITOR.

The monitor stared back.

Well, maybe it didn't stare back, but it seemed to Rhodes that the machine was looking at him. It had one big eye, like the Purple People Eater from the old song, and it reminded Rhodes of the rumors that used to circulate through his grade school classes about the speaker at the front of the room. The principal made the daily announcements over the speaker system, but everyone said that the speaker worked both ways and that the principal could listen in on the classroom if he wanted to.

Rhodes had always believed that story, and he wondered who might be watching him through the monitor. Then he shook his head. He knew he was being silly. Still . . . .

"It's great, ain't it?" Hack Jensen said.

Hack, tall and lean, with a pencil-thin mustache that was mostly gray, was the dispatcher for the Blacklin County Sheriff's Department, a man well past the usual retirement age, who relished the fact that he at long last had the computer that he had been insisting was a necessity for several years.

"Too bad it took that million-dollar lawsuit for us to get one of these things," Hack went on when Rhodes did not respond to his question.

Hack, Rhodes, and Lawton, the jailor, along with the county, had been sued for a million dollars by one of the jail's former inmates. The jail had passed its inspection, however, and an architectural firm had certified that it was structurally sound. The county commissioners had decided that a few things did need improvement, nevertheless, and the computer was one of the first fruits of the new funds that had been allotted to the Sheriff's Department.

"I guess it's all right," Rhodes said at last, not absolutely sure how he felt about the computer. He liked technology in general, but the department had gotten along for years without a computer. He still wasn't certain they really needed one.

There it was, though, sitting on a new prefab computer desk that had been set up beside the old desk Hack had been using for his radio and telephone. There were a keyboard, a monitor, a printer, and a rectangular box that Rhodes supposed held all the chips and disks and whatever else it was that a computer needed to function.

"All right?" Hack said. "Is that all you got to say? Why, in about a minute this thing can tell us all kinds of stuff that would've taken us a week to get the old way."

"What kind of stuff?" Lawton said, coming in from the cellblock.

Lawton was Lou Costello to Hack's Bud Abbott. He was short and chubby, with a smooth, cherubic face that belied his years.

"Stuff we need to know," Hack said. He pointed to the monitor. "Look here. We can tap into NCIC and get—"

"Wait a minute," Rhodes said. "NCIC. What's that?"

Hack snorted with disgust. He had watched every minute of the installation of the computer and had studied the manuals diligently. The county had paid for a consultant to come in and demonstrate its operation, but Hack was the only one who had sat in on the sessions. He prided himself on knowing the lingo.

"If you'd listened to that little guy who came and explained ever'thing to us, you'd know about NCIC," Hack said.

Rhodes didn't say anything. He'd had other things to do. He'd just gotten married, for one thing, and he'd gone to Mexico on his honeymoon. For another, he didn't have the luxury of being in the office all the time, as Hack did.

"NCIC means National Crime Information Center," Hack said. "All you got to do is give the name and date of birth, and you get a complete criminal history. Arrests, outstandin' warrants, all that stuff. And then there's TCIC—"

"TCIC?" Lawton said.

Hack looked at him with contempt. "*Texas* Crime Information Center. Gives you just the stuff from this state. You know what state we're in, don't you?"

"Course I do," Lawton said. "I just don't see how that little machine knows all that."

"It's not just this machine," Rhodes said. He knew that much. "We're hooked into Austin some way. There's a bigger machine there."

"Through the phone lines," Hack said. "We're hooked in through the phone lines."

"Is that all it does?" Lawton said. He wasn't impressed, or if he was, he wasn't going to admit it.

Hack shook his head sadly. "No, that's not all," he said. "We can get to the Department of Public Safety, too. If I type in a license plate number, I can find out who owns a car, or if it's stolen, or who's got the lien on it. I can find out how old the plates are—"

"Who'd want to know that?" Lawton said.

"*I* don't know. It's just one of the things you can find out.

Used to, if we wanted to know who owned a car with a certain number, we had to go to the courthouse and—"

"Yeah, I know," Lawton said. "Go through the records, all that."

"Yeah. So you can see what a help it'll be."

"I guess so," Lawton said. "If it works."

That was one thing that had been worrying Rhodes. The old methods had been slow, but they were dependable.

"It works," Hack said. "Watch this."

He typed in Lawton's full name.

"When were you born?" he said.

"It ain't none of your business," Lawton said.

"You might as well tell me. I can look it up anyway."

"Can't find it on that machine, huh?"

"Sure I can. But this machine'll give me ever'body with your same name unless I can narrow it down first. Now go ahead and tell me."

Lawton stalled for a minute, then gave in. "November fifth, nineteen and twenty."

Hack typed it in.

They waited, watching the monitor. Then the information appeared on the screen, just as it appeared on Lawton's driver's license: height, color of hair and eyes, address, license number, category of license, and the expiration date.

"No outstandin' warrants," Hack said. "Looks like you ain't got much of a record. Not countin' that speedin' ticket you got back in the fall. Huh. I don't remember you tellin' us about any speedin' ticket."

"Lemme see that," Lawton said, leaning in closer to the screen. "I'll be damn'. I'd forgot that myself. Highway Patrol got me for doin' forty-five in a thirty-five zone. I tried to talk 'im out of it, but he wouldn't listen." He continued to stare at the screen. "I guess that thing's smarter than I thought."

"It ain't smart," Hack said. "It's the one who operates it that has to be smart."

Lawton turned his gaze to Hack. "And that means you, I guess."

"You guess right."

Rhodes headed off the argument. "I'm looking forward to seeing how it works when we really need it. You're right, Hack. It could be a real help."

Hack didn't try to hide the look of smug satisfaction on his face. "That's what I been tellin' you," he said.

"I know," Rhodes said. "I know."

Hack might have gone on at length about how he had been trying for just about forever to get a computer for the department, but they were interrupted by the opening of the jail door.

The raw and gusty wind came out of the March night and ripped the door out of the grip of the man who stood there watching them and slammed it back against the wall with a loud crash. Papers rustled on desks all over the room.

The man turned hurriedly and grabbed the edge of the door, pushing it closed.

"I'm sorry," he said. "I didn't mean to—"

"It's all right," Rhodes said. "We're used to it."

They were. The pneumatic closer had worn out quite a while before and had not yet been fixed or replaced. The wind had been tearing the door from the grasp of about every third person who entered the jail for the past two days. The use of paperweights was becoming a habit.

"It's just that I'm a little nervous," the man said.

Rhodes thought the man looked nervous, all right. He was slightly built, about five feet two inches tall, with mild blue eyes and drooping lids that made him look just the least bit sleepy, as if he'd just been waked from a nap, though his eyes darted alertly around the office. He had fine brown hair that the wind had distributed over his head like straw.

"Just have a seat over by my desk," Rhodes said, indicating the chair. "Then you can tell me what's bothering you."

Rhodes wondered who the man was. Blacklin County was small, but he didn't know everyone in it, not by a long shot. Still, he'd have bet this man was from somewhere else. It was his clothes, mostly. He wore an expensive suit and shoes that looked even costlier. About the highest-priced shoes you could buy in Clearview, which was where the jail was located and the biggest town in the county, were Florsheims. And while they could cost you up over a hundred dollars, a hundred dollars still wouldn't get you into the same neighborhood as the shoes the little man was wearing.

"I can tell you without sitting down," the man said, running a hand through his hair and trying to get it back in place. "What's bothering me is ghosts."

"Ghosts?" Rhodes said.

Hack and Lawton, who had been feigning interest in the computer, dropped all pretense at not listening. Hack turned his chair to face the stranger, and Lawton braced his ample rear end against Hack's computer desk. Hack gave him an elbow, and he moved silently to the radio desk.

The man laughed unconvincingly. "I know it sounds strange." He looked over at the chair Rhodes had indicated. "Maybe you're right. Maybe I should sit down."

He moved over to the chair and sat. His feet reached the floor, but just barely. Rhodes sat at his desk and looked at him, waiting.

"My name is Hal Brame," the man said.

He reached into his suit and drew out a leather card case, removed a card and handed it to Rhodes, who knew for sure now that he wasn't dealing with a local. He couldn't think of anyone in the entire county who carried business cards, much less a card case.

Rhodes looked at the card and ran his thumb idly over the engraving. Then he got his half-moon reading glasses out of his shirt pocket so that he could read it.

HAL BRAME

DEALER IN FINE BOOKS

USED AND RARE

There was a Houston address, and the telephone number in the lower right-hand corner had the Houston area code, 713.

"Well, Mr. Brame," Rhodes said, putting the card on his cluttered desk and slipping the glasses back into his pocket. "What's this about ghosts?"

The man gave his unconvincing laugh again. "I know it sounds crazy. But the effect of those old buildings at night is startling, to say the least. I'm not usually frightened so easily, but—"

"Wait a minute," Rhodes said. "Maybe you'd better start at the beginning. What old buildings are you talking about?"

Brame sighed. "I'm sorry. My mind just isn't working properly. I'm usually a very well organized person. Give me a moment, please." He closed his eyes and took a deep breath, letting it out very slowly.

Hack nudged Lawton and gave him a significant look, but neither of them said anything. Rhodes waited patiently until Brame had composed himself.

After a minute Brame opened his eyes. "I deal in rare books, as you can see," he said. "I drove up to a little town called Obert after I closed my shop today, to meet with Simon Graham. He owns the college there."

Rhodes knew about Graham. Several years before, he had bought an abandoned college campus in Obert. The campus was not large, consisting of the main building, a dormitory, a gymnasium, and several houses where faculty and administrators had lived. None of the buildings had been used in more than twenty-five years, but the college had a long history. It had been established as a church school not long after the Civil War, and though the buildings had changed hands several times, it had continued to operate under the guidance of one denomination or another until around 1960. After that, it had gone out of operation and the campus had slowly deteriorated over the years.

Simon Graham had bought the place with the intention of restoring the buildings and making them into some kind of tourist attraction, research institute, and historical site. The main building, which was the only building remaining from the original campus, was to become a museum, and the dormitory was to be a bed-and-breakfast inn. It would have been quite a benefit to the community of Obert, had Graham's plans come to fruition, but so far they had not.

"Simon and I are in the same business, more or less," Brame said. "Rare books. Of course, he operates on a much larger scale than I do, as you probably know."

Rhodes knew, but only vaguely. There were rumors that Graham had somehow become enormously wealthy by dealing in books, something that Rhodes found hard to understand.

"He called to tell me that he had a first edition of *Tamerlane and Other Poems* for sale," Brame said. He held up his right hand, palm outward as if to ward off a protest from his listeners. "I know. I know. You don't believe it. And I didn't either. Copies are so seldom available, and then only at auction. But one never knows. It was something I simply had to check out, so I drove up."

"Up to Obert," Rhodes said.

"Yes. It's a very small place, isn't it."

"Maybe two hundred people if you count the ones on the farms around it," Rhodes said.

"Yes. There was only one store that I saw, and a post office. And not very many lights in the houses. It was very lonesome up on that hill."

Rhodes could understand how Brame felt, coming from Houston where there were traffic and lights at all hours of the night. Up on Obert's Hill, where the college campus was located, it would seem very quiet and dark to a city boy.

"I located Simon's house," Brame said, "or at least I think it was his house. It was right next to one of the college buildings."

"That's where he lives," Rhodes said. "In the old President's House. It's the only one that's been fully restored."

"That was the place, then," Brame said. "But there was no one there. I knocked and knocked, but no one came, and there were no lights."

"People go to bed early in the country," Hack said from across the room.

"Yes, I'm sure they do," Brame said. "But then I noticed lights in the old main building."

"Are you sure?" Rhodes said. "I don't think there's been too much work done on it since they gutted it."

"I wouldn't know about that," Brame said. "All I know is what I saw."

"Lights," Rhodes said.

"Yes, but not lights like the ones you have in here. Not room lights. These lights were moving. I could see them through the windows."

"Oh," Rhodes said. He had a feeling they were getting to the point now. "You mean like flashlights."

"No," Brame said. "I don't mean like flashlights, at least not like flashlights held by normal people. I'm not a flighty person, Sheriff, but what I saw gave me a shiver. That's why I'm here."

"All right," Rhodes said. "Tell me what you saw."

"Very well. The lights were moving, as I said, but not as if they were being carried. One of them rose through the air very quickly until it was quite high up. Then it spun around and around and shot across the room. I could see it flying past several of the windows. Then it went out."

"And you thought about ghosts," Rhodes said.

Brame nodded. "Yes. But it wasn't just the lights that made me think that way."

"What else was there?"

"There were the noises."

"What kind of noises?"

"Just . . . noises. I wouldn't call them screams, but they could have been. Very loud groans, perhaps."

"Like the noises a ghost might make," Rhodes said.

Brame looked at him to see if he might be poking fun, but Rhodes's face was serious.

"Yes," Brame said. "Like the noises a ghost might make. I know it's not ghosts, of course, but something strange is going on out there. So I drove back here and asked where the Sheriff's Office was."

"You did the right thing," Rhodes said. "I guess we'll have to go out there and have a look. What kind of car are you driving?"

"A black Volvo," Brame said.

That would have cinched it even if it hadn't been for the clothes. No one in Blacklin County owned a Volvo.

"All right," Rhodes said. "I'll follow you out there."

"Very well," Brame said. He got up. "Shall I get started?"

"Go ahead," Rhodes said. "I'll catch up with you."

Hack and Lawton watched Brame walk to the door. This time he got a good grip on it, and the wind didn't have a chance to shove it inward.

"Fancy little fella, ain't he?" Hack said when the door closed behind Brame.

"Yeah," Lawton said. "You reckon your computer can get in touch with the GCIC?"

"GCIC?" Hack said.

"Ghost Criminal Investigation Center," Lawton said.

"God-dang you, Lawton," Hack said. "It ain't somethin' to joke about."

Lawton laughed. "I'll tell you what else ain't somethin' to joke about."

Hack's anger died out as quickly as it had appeared. "What's that?"

Lawton gestured to Rhodes. "Havin' to call your new wife and tell her you won't be home anytime soon."

Rhodes looked at the telephone on his desk. Ivy had understood when she married him that he kept irregular hours, but that didn't make calling her any easier.

"You want me and Hack to go lock ourselves in a cell for a while?" Lawton said. "Let you have a little privacy?"

"No," Rhodes said. "You don't need to do that."

He reached for the phone.

2

RHODES FOLLOWED BRAME'S BLACK VOLVO OUT THE OBERT road. The sky was heavily overcast, the night totally black, and the wind buffeted the county car. The tops of the trees by the roadside thrashed and twisted in the dark rush of air.

For two days the wind had blown from the north, bringing with it unseasonably cold weather. Rhodes knew that the county was going through the dreaded "Easter spell." Every year it would seem that spring had arrived, with sunny days, singing birds, and blue skies; but every year Hack and Lawton would prophesy that there would be one more bad stretch of weather before summer. They called it the "Easter spell." It was their conviction that the bad weather always coincided with the Easter weekend, and they were always correct, at least in their own opinions.

The fact that it was not Easter now, and that it would not be Easter for another two weeks, did not bother them. Any bad weather that came within two weeks of Easter was the Easter spell, and that was that. Rhodes had tried to argue that an *Easter* spell could come only at Easter, but they merely shook their heads in pity at his lack of understanding when it came to authentic weather lore.

Obert was not far, only about eight miles west of Clearview, and in a short time Rhodes was pulling up beside the Volvo in a graveled parking space near the main building of the college campus. Nearby there was a historical marker that gave some information about the college's founding and about the construction of the main building, which was built of hand-cut native stone. Although Rhodes could not read the marker in the dark, he knew what it said; he'd seen it several times before.

He got out of the county car and looked around, the wind tearing at his jacket and pants. Because Obert's Hill was one of the highest points between Houston and Dallas, it was also one of the windiest. On a clear day you could see for quite a distance from up there, but on a dark night like this no one would have known that.

The side of the main building loomed in front of Rhodes. The dark hulk was three stories tall, not counting the attic space. Considering that each floor had sixteen-foot ceilings, the building was impressively tall, easily one of the tallest in the county. No light glinted from the many windows, a lot of which were probably missing their panes.

Brame walked over and stood beside Rhodes.

"Where did you see the lights?" Rhodes said.

"In there," Brame said. He stood almost at an angle, as if bracing himself against the wind, which was so strong Rhodes was surprised that it didn't just pick Brame up and carry him away.

"Where in there?"

"On the third floor."

"The third floor?" Rhodes said. Brame hadn't mentioned that little fact earlier.

"Yes. My car was parked just about where it is now. I got out and walked to that house over there." He pointed toward a freshly painted frame house that had probably been constructed in the 1920s, making it not nearly as old as the main building. "I knocked on the door, but no one came.

I waited for a while, and then I came back to the car. That's when I saw the lights."

Rhodes was looking toward the house. There was an unattached garage about twenty yards away and to the back. There was some kind of vehicle parked in the garage, but Rhodes couldn't tell what it was.

"Was there a car in the garage when you knocked?" he said.

Brame couldn't remember. He probably hadn't even looked.

"There's one there now," Rhodes said. "We'd better try the house again. Mr. Graham's probably just been out for a while."

Rhodes got a flashlight out of his car, and he and Brame walked over to the house. Rhodes noticed again how short Brame was. Rhodes was about six feet, which he didn't consider tall, not in Texas, but he towered over the book dealer.

Rhodes shined the light into the garage when they got to the house. There was a black Ford Lariat pickup parked inside. Rhodes could read a sticker on the chrome bumper: "NEXT TO SEX, I LIKE LAS VEGAS BEST."

They stepped up on the porch. The house was dark, but Rhodes knocked on the door facing. There was no answer from inside. They waited for a minute, then Rhodes knocked again. There was no answer that time, either.

"Those could have been prowlers that you saw in the main building," Rhodes told Brame. "I guess that's justification enough for me to enter. Maybe you'd better wait for me out here."

Brame looked around. His face was a pale blur. "If it's all the same to you, Sheriff, I think I'd like to come along. I don't much like the idea of being out here all alone."

"Okay," Rhodes said. "Come on."

They left the porch of the house and walked around to the front of the main building. In spite of the fact that it wasn't really spring yet, the grass was already in need of trimming and thick-stemmed weeds were proliferating.

The building was fronted by a long porch covered by a roof two stories above. The porch was lined with wooden columns that were really no more than four-by-fours. Rhodes wondered what had happened to the original columns.

Because the building had been erected long before anyone had thought about air-conditioning, there were high windows lining the front just as there were on the sides and back. Most of them were covered by tattered and rusting screens. There was a screen door in front of the wooden entrance door. The screen was closed, but the entrance door was slightly ajar.

"He hasn't really kept the place up very well, has he?" Brame said.

"No," Rhodes said, wondering about the door. He knew a little about the plans Graham had for the campus, since those plans had a tangential connection with an earlier murder case, and it was true that most of Graham's grandiose schemes had never been realized. He had fixed up the house he lived in, but very little had ever been done to the other buildings. Even that didn't account for the door's being open, however.

"I wonder if he'll ever finish this project?" Brame said. "It doesn't seem as if he's gotten very far."

Rhodes didn't answer. He pulled open the screen door and shined his light inside.

There was nothing much to see. No desks, no blackboards, no offices, no sign that the building had ever served as an educational institution. Only the main support walls remained, and the stairway.

"The door's open," Rhodes said. "That could mean that someone's inside, or that someone's been inside recently." He was saying it as much for the record as anything, just in case his reason for entering the building ever came up. "I'll go inside and investigate." He looked at Brame. "You still want to come with me?"

"Not really," Brame said. "But I don't want to stand out here, either."

Rhodes didn't particularly blame him. The wind moaned around the old building and sang through its cracks and crevices. It shook and rattled the window panes. It was almost enough to make a man believe in ghosts, all right.

Rhodes went inside, shining his light ahead of him, chasing shadows across the floor. He was followed closely by the book dealer.

The stairs were covered by ragged carpeting that had needed replacement at the time the school closed so long before. It had not improved in the interval. It was a faded green, thick with dust.

"Walk over on this side," Rhodes said, ascending next to the wall. He didn't really expect that there might be footprints in the dusty carpet, but if there were they would probably be in the middle of the steps or on the side by the railing.

They stopped on the second floor, and Rhodes shined the light around. There were a few pieces of lumber on the floor, but they looked as if they had been there for years.

They went on up.

The third floor was different. It had been used as the chapel in the earliest days of the college, and there were no walls. The entire floor was one large room, and at one time there had been benches for the students to sit on while they received their daily dose of religion.

Now the floor was covered with boards, ropes, paint buckets, and disassembled scaffolding. The smell of paint lingered in the air. The restoration work, such as it was, had obviously begun on this floor.

Rhodes shined the light around carefully. It reflected back at him from window panes that had loosened in their frames over the years. They clattered in the wind.

"There doesn't seem to be anyone up here," Rhodes said. He couldn't see any place in the room where someone could be hiding.

Brame seemed relieved. "Good. I was afraid—yaaaahhhh!"

The book dealer yelled and jumped so high that his head was nearly on a level with Rhodes's own.

"What's that?" Brame screamed, pointing into the darkness with one hand. The other was clutching Rhodes's sleeve.

Rhodes swung the flashlight beam and it caught a rat scuttling across the back of the large room, looking for a place to hide. Dust motes stirred by the rat's feet floated up through the beam of the flashlight. The rat disappeared behind a row of paint cans and collapsed scaffolding.

"He won't bother us," Rhodes said. He was about to turn and leave when for some reason he glanced up.

There was no ceiling on the room, just the bare rafters of the attic. The wind whined through small holes in the roof that had not been repaired and through which stars might have been visible on a different night. At the end of the room where the rat had disappeared, high in the dark, something moved.

Rhodes turned the light upward. It twinkled off the silver toe covers of a pair of cowboy boots before being absorbed by dark blue cloth. As the light moved up higher, Rhodes could see that a man's body was dangling from the rafters.

"Jesus Christ," Brame said.

The light hit the man's face.

"It's Simon," Brame said. "Jesus Christ, it's Simon."

Rhodes had never met Simon Graham, but he had heard enough about the man to know that although he was a native of New Jersey, he always dressed like a professional Texan, and the man in the light's beam certainly fit that part of the description. He was wearing the boots with their silver toe covers, boot-cut jeans, a dark shirt with a black string tie. He wasn't wearing a hat.

There was a hangman's noose around his neck, and his head was twisted at an odd angle. It was practically touching the rafter high above.

Rhodes followed the rope with his light. The other end was tied around the knob of a door in the back wall. Rhodes told himself that he should have noticed the rope before, but he'd been looking for prowlers, not a hanged man, and he'd only half believed Brame's story in the first place.

He believed it now, though. Or at least he believed *something* had gone on in the old building. He still wasn't buying into the bit about the ghosts.

Brame was breathing hard, taking deep gulping breaths. "I never saw a dead man before," he said between gulps.

"I'll have to call in," Rhodes said. "Do you want to come down with me?"

"You bet I do," Brame said.

Two hours later, Graham had been declared dead by the justice of the peace, his body had been removed, and Rhodes, along with Deputy Ruth Grady, had set up portable lighting and done a thorough search of the room.

Among other things they had found Graham's hat, a genuine gray Stetson, behind a stack of lumber not far from where he was hanging. He had probably shaken it off. And they had found a flashlight partially submerged in a paint can.

"Do you think he threw it in there?" Ruth said. She was short and compact, a good officer, and had studied police science in a community college.

"I don't think he could have done it if he'd been trying," Rhodes said. He recounted Brame's story of what he had seen through the windows. "He would have been struggling as he died, maybe spinning around, and the light could have flown out of his hands. It just happened to land in a can of paint."

"So he decided at the last he didn't want to die," Ruth said. She had thought from the first that they were dealing with a suicide.

Rhodes wasn't so sure.

"But it looks as if he stood on the scaffolding," Ruth said. "Then he put the noose over his head and kicked the scaffolding over."

It could have happened that way. The boards and metal joints of scaffolding were lying about where they would have fallen if Graham had done exactly what Ruth said.

"Maybe," Rhodes said. "Or maybe someone just wanted it to look that way to us."

Ruth admitted that he might have a point. "I guess we go on the assumption that it's murder, then."

Rhodes told her that they wouldn't make any assumptions just yet. "We'll have to find out what we can from whatever we find here, and then get busy asking questions. I don't see much that's going to help us." He looked at the scaffolding, the paint cans, the rope.

Ruth said she hoped she could get some prints off the part of the flashlight's handle that had not been in the paint and maybe some of the metal parts of the scaffolding. She wasn't so hopeful about the rope.

Other than those three things, there seemed to be no sign that anyone had been in the room. The dust on the floor had been disturbed by the work that had gone on there recently, but there was nothing to indicate any other kind of disturbance.

"There doesn't look as if there was much of a struggle," Ruth said, still pursuing the suicide angle. "What would anyone else be doing up here? And why would anyone want to kill Simon Graham? Maybe it *is* just a simple suicide."

Rhodes wasn't so sure that killing yourself was ever simple, but he smiled. "Answer those two questions, and you'll have it all wrapped up."

He was wondering the same things himself, of course. He was also wondering about Brame, who had been adamant about wanting to return to the scene. Rhodes had not allowed him to do so, despite Brame's loud insistence.

"There are things you might not understand," Brame had said. Then, realizing how that sounded, he said, "I mean, I'm a dealer in rare books, like Simon was. I can help you with your investigation."

"If I need your help, and I'm sure I will, I'll call on you," Rhodes told him. "In the meantime, you should get a room at a motel for the night. We can talk again tomorrow."

Brame persisted for a while, but it eventually became obvious to him that Rhodes was not going to let him back inside the building. He finally got into his Volvo and drove away.

It was much later than Rhodes had thought it would be when he left Obert for home. He drove through the tiny town and made the wide curve that led down the hill. It was too dark to see the bluebonnets that were just beginning to bloom on the roadside.

On the way back to Clearview he passed a deserted service station/grocery that a sign proclaimed to be THE KOUNTRY STOAR. He wondered briefly what had happened to Miss Bobbitt, who had once been engaged to the store's owner. She had left Clearview two weeks previously, without telling anyone where she was going. Good riddance, as far as Rhodes was concerned.

He looked at the dashboard clock. It was after midnight. He wondered if Ivy would be waiting up for him.

3

WHEN RHODES'S FIRST WIFE HAD DIED OF CANCER SOME YEARS before, he had thought he would never marry again, if he thought of marriage at all. Meeting Ivy Daniel in the course of a murder investigation, however, had changed his mind. It had taken a while, but he had come around to accepting the fact that getting married again might not be such a bad idea after all.

Even then, he had not married immediately. Ivy had a few doubts of her own, especially about his job. Nights like this were one cause of those doubts.

Rhodes pulled the county car into his driveway. There was light coming from the living room, which meant that Ivy had not gone to bed. He didn't know whether that was a bad sign or a good one.

Rhodes parked and walked through the backyard. There were almost as many weeds in it as there were around the college buildings. Rhodes hated yard work, and he wondered if he could find a high-school kid to do the mowing.

While he was wondering about that, Speedo, whose real name was Mr. Earl, bounded up and put his paws on Rhodes's chest. Speedo could always be counted on for a friendly greeting, no matter how late Rhodes came home. This was another relationship that Rhodes had established in the course of the same investigation during which he had met Ivy, though Speedo had moved in long before Ivy did.

Rhodes gave Speedo's head a good rub and checked the food and water bowls before going into the house.

Ivy was sitting on the couch in a maroon velour robe. She was watching a late movie, and Rhodes glanced at the TV screen as he entered the room.

He recognized Gail Russell in a scene from *Angel and the Badman.* It wasn't the colorized version.

"Hi," Ivy said. "Does the name of this movie give you any ideas?"

"Maybe," Rhodes said. "Which one of us is supposed to be the badman?"

"I thought that was obvious," Ivy said, standing up and walking over to him.

It was. On their honeymoon in Cozumel, Ivy had looked better in her bathing suit than most of the women half her age. Rhodes, on the other hand, had spent a lot of his time wishing that he had ridden his stationary bike more often and wondering how high above his waist he could reasonably pull his own suit. If he pulled it high enough, he could almost fool himself into believing his stomach was flat. The tape on his damaged ribs hadn't helped things any, either.

"I'm sorry I'm so late," he said.

"Why? I knew you were a minion of the law when I married you. Want a Dr Pepper?"

Rhodes realized that not only was he thirsty, he hadn't eaten supper. "Sure," he said, thankful that there was no problem, and they went into the kitchen.

One thing that had bothered Rhodes about remarrying was the memories connected with this house and the rooms in it, memories of the way Clare had smiled, of things she had said, of the way she had moved through the house. He had worried that those memories might interfere with Ivy's happiness, and maybe even with his own.

That had not turned out to be the case, however. The memories were there, of course, and most of them were good ones, but they were not overpowering. They lingered in the back of his mind, always there, but they were only memories, a part of the past. Ivy was the here and now.

She opened the refrigerator and got out a Dr Pepper in a twelve-ounce glass bottle. That was one big change in his domestic arrangements, right there. While living alone, Rhodes had bought his soft drinks, when he remembered to do it, in two-liter plastic containers or in cans. He much preferred the taste of Dr Pepper out of glass bottles, but you couldn't get them in convenience stores, and it was too much trouble to actually shop for them, at least for him. Ivy didn't seem to mind.

"Have you eaten anything?" Ivy said. She had become familiar with Rhodes's catch-as-catch-can eating habits.

"Nope," Rhodes said. He took a swallow of the Dr Pepper.

"I didn't think so. I'll warm up some meat loaf."

That was another big change. Rhodes had for years lived mostly on Dr Pepper, bologna sandwiches, cheese crackers, and whatever fast food he could pick up. It had always puzzled him that he could gain weight on such a diet, but he had managed to do it. He had bought a stationary bicycle with the honorable intention of getting more exercise, but he rarely had a chance to ride it.

He was sure that he was going to gain even more weight now, since Ivy actually cooked occasionally. She had a job of her own in an insurance office, and she had no intention of giving it up, but neither did she intend to adapt her own eating habits to Rhodes's unhealthy ways. She even had him eating high-fiber cereal for breakfast. At least she hadn't made him give up Dr Pepper.

While Rhodes was eating the meat loaf, he told Ivy about

the night's events. She wasn't quite accustomed as yet to talking about things like suicide and/or murder over warmed-up meat loaf, but as usual she was interested in Rhodes's job and ready to discuss it with him. And as it turned out, she knew a lot more about Simon Graham than Rhodes did.

"He's not very well liked in antiquarian book circles," she said, sitting across from him at the round oak table. "Most of those people really love books. He's thought of as more of a wheeler-dealer who could just as well be selling used cars or insurance. And some people think he might be a little on the shady side."

Rhodes pushed back his empty plate. "How do you know so much about him?" he said.

"There was a profile of him in one of the Sunday supplements a few weeks ago," Ivy said. "I read it."

Rhodes nodded. He didn't have time for much reading, though he always tried to read the comics section. He thought it was at least as relevant to life as the front page. Maybe more.

"Tell me more about the 'shady' part," he said.

Ivy looked up and off to the left, remembering. "There was something about forged books," she said. "Could that be right? I know that people can forge checks, but how could anyone forge a book?"

Rhodes didn't know. "Why would anyone want to?" he said. That was something he'd have to talk to Brame about.

"Because they're worth a lot of money, some of them. Not the ones you can find on the rack at Wal-Mart, but the old ones, and even some fairly recent first editions, like some of the early Stephen King books."

"And that's how Graham made his money, selling Stephen King books?"

"Not exactly. The books he usually dealt in were a lot older, but he'd sell anything, even Stephen King books if he could get them. That's what some people didn't like about him. He really didn't care much about books, or so some people said. He just knew what would bring a good price, how to promote himself, and how to call attention to his business."

"By dressing like a drugstore cowboy," Rhodes put in. He knew about that.

"That was part of it," Ivy agreed. "But there was more to it than that. He knew how to spend money, too. He gave a lot of parties, served the best food, poured the best drinks, and invited all the best people."

"He didn't invite me."

Ivy laughed. Rhodes liked the sound of it.

"He probably would have invited you if he'd had the parties around here, but he didn't. He had them in Houston. That's where he lives, after all. Or where he did live, if that was really him you found tonight."

"I had the impression he lived in Obert," Rhodes said. "On the old college grounds."

"He has a house there. Had. Whatever. But he lived in Houston most of the time, not in Obert. Houston's where he had his bookstore. You can't be a big-time antiquarian book dealer in a place like Obert."

"Not even if you have your own personal college?" Rhodes said.

"There was something about that in the article, too. Some people said that buying the college in Obert was just another one of Graham's big publicity schemes and that nothing would ever come of it."

"Another one? What were some of the others?"

"He was connected to horse racing in some way. He was one of the backers of a track that was supposed to get organized out in Harris County. It never happened."

Rhodes didn't see anything unusual in that. Since the state legislature had approved pari-mutuel betting in Texas a couple of years before, only one track had gotten under way. That one was in a small town out near Brownwood, and it had gone bankrupt.

"Some people think he lost a lot of money in that deal and a few others," Ivy said. "There were rumors that he was almost addicted to gambling and that he bet heavily at some of the Eastern tracks and lost just as heavily. He loved playing blackjack in Las Vegas and Atlantic City."

Rhodes remembered the bumper sticker he had seen on the vehicle in Graham's garage.

"There was some question as to whether he was as rich as people thought he was," Ivy went on. "People said he owed so much money to the bookies and to the casinos that he would never be able to pay it all."

So Graham might have had reasons to kill himself, Rhodes thought. Money was always a reason, and the rumors about forgery might be reasons as well. People in high positions, either in society or business, did not like to see their reputations shattered by accusations of wrongdoing. Especially if the accusations could be shown to be true.

"Did he ever do anything right?" Rhodes said.

"He did manage quite a few coups in his book dealings," Ivy said. "I don't remember all the details, but I think some of those deals were suspect because of the forgery angle."

"I guess we've thrown away the paper that had that article in it," Rhodes said.

"Probably. But the library would have a copy. Do you want any more meat loaf?"

Rhodes looked at the clock on top of the refrigerator. Nearly one-thirty. "I don't think so," he said. "Time for bed. I've got to get an early start in the morning."

"How early?"

"Not *that* early," Rhodes said, smiling.

Rhodes went by Ballinger's Funeral Home before going to the jail the next morning. He wanted to talk to Ballinger about the body of Simon Graham.

The Easter spell had blown itself out, and the sky was a brilliant clear blue. It was going to be a beautiful day, not the kind of day to be worrying about a murder. But, then, what day was?

Ballinger was an early riser, and he was sitting in his office in the small building behind the funeral home when Rhodes drove up. He did not fit the general public's stereotyped idea of a funeral director who spent his life in a state of perpetual gloom, and he met Rhodes at the door with his usual smile.

He was holding a paperback book in his left hand, and that wasn't unusual, either. He frequented the local garage sales looking for old paperback mysteries. Rhodes looked down at the book and tried to read the title.

Seeing where Rhodes was looking, Ballinger brought the book up to eye level. "Shoot It Again, Sam," he said. "Michael Avallone. He wrote just about everything— books about 'The Man from U.N.C.L.E.,' books about somebody called 'The Satan Sleuth,' hell, he even wrote books about 'The Partridge Family.' You oughta read this one, though, as much as you like old movies. I think this Avallone fella must like 'em, too. There's this private eye, see, named Ed Noon—"

"What about that man that was brought in last night?" Rhodes said. He hated to interrupt Ballinger, but if you let him get started on his favorite topic, he was likely to run on for hours.

"Simon Graham," Ballinger said, lowering the book. "You better come on in."

They went inside the office. There were shelves lined with paperbacks, and Rhodes wondered if Graham had ever collected books like that. Probably not.

"Dr. White came by," Ballinger said, sitting behind his desk and putting the paperback down on it after marking his place with a slip of paper. "You'll be getting a report."

"I know," Rhodes said, sitting in a chair facing the desk. "But you talked to him, didn't you?"

Ballinger not only had his office in the small building they were in; he lived there, ready for any emergency, day or night. He would have known when the body came in.

"Sure," he said. "I talk to everybody."

"What did you find out?"

"Well, he didn't die easy, that's for sure. You know, when they hung you in the old days, they'd spring the trap and you'd drop down, and that noose would break your neck. That's why it's tied that way and why the hangman had to get the knot just in the right place by your ear. Supposed to be a kind of merciful way to go if it was done right. But if you just strangle to death, which is apparently what happened to Graham, well, you don't go so easy."

"Dr. White thinks that's what happened? Graham strangled?"

"Looks that way. There're some scratches on Graham's face and neck where he tried to get the rope off, and there was some skin under his fingernails. Probably his. His hands and fingers were a little raw, too. Tried to hold himself up, take his weight off the rope. Shirttail all pulled out. No doubt that he strangled."

"He didn't kill himself, then," Rhodes said.

"Dr. White didn't say that. Even a man who kills himself can change his mind at the last minute."

"Dr. White kept the fingernail scrapings for me?"

"They're here. Tagged and bagged. I'll get 'em for you before you leave. They're all ready to go to the lab if you want to send 'em."

Ninety-nine chances out of a hundred, the skin under the fingernails did indeed come from Graham's own neck and face, but Rhodes would send the scrapings to the lab anyway, just in case.

"What about the time of death?"

Ballinger told him. The time that Dr. White estimated fit the facts as Rhodes knew them so far.

"Anything else?" he said.

Ballinger shook his head. "Not that he told me. You'll get it all in the report, though."

"Thanks," Rhodes said, standing up.

"I'll walk you to the car, get you those bags," Ballinger said, standing also. "You know, Sheriff, this is likely to be a pretty big case. Graham was a wealthy man, and he was pretty well known over the state. This is going to get coverage in the big-city papers."

Just what I need, Rhodes thought. "I hope they haven't found out about it yet," he said. "We're still trying to locate the next of kin."

In fact, Ruth was supposed to call two people the previous evening. Neither of them was related to Graham, but their numbers had been in his wallet. One of them was a woman named Marty Wallace; the other was a man, Mitch Rolingson, who was Graham's business partner. There was no way Rhodes could control what those two might have done.

"I haven't called anybody, if that's what you mean," Ballinger said. His feelings were hurt. "I'd never do a thing like that, call the reporters about a death."

"Not even Red Rogers?" Rhodes said. Rogers was the name used on the air by a local radio reporter, Larry Redden.

Ballinger smiled. He knew that Rhodes had experienced a run-in or two with Redden in the past. "You know better than that."

Rhodes nodded. "Just checking. Let's go get those bags."

"The boys from the eight-seven would eat this up," Ballinger said as they went outside. Another of his enthusiasms was Ed McBain's series of books about the lives and jobs of the cops in a fictional big city much like New York. "A deal like this, I bet the Deaf Man would be in it some way. If he murdered somebody like that, he'd do a good job of making it look like suicide or something."

"Did Dr. White say anything about murder?" Rhodes said.

"No," Ballinger said. "I was just thinking how the Deaf Man would do things."

Rhodes had heard about the Deaf Man from Ballinger before. "Isn't he the one who sends clues for the police to figure out?"

"That's the one," Ballinger said.

"Then he's not involved," Rhodes said.

4

WHEN RHODES GOT TO THE JAIL, HE OPENED THE DOOR CARE-
fully, but to his surprise the pneumatic opener worked just
exactly as it was supposed to.

"Ruth fixed it," Hack said. He was looking at the monitor. Lawton was sweeping the floor.

Rhodes came on into the office. Hack had been very
suspicious of a woman deputy at first, but Ruth had turned
out to be very good at her job. And she could fix things, too.
It had not taken Hack long to begin thinking very highly of
her.

"What are you looking at?" Rhodes said.

"Simon Graham's criminal history," Hack said.

Rhodes was surprised. "He's got one?"

Hack turned away from the screen. "Naw. Just a lotta
speedin' tickets that he ain't paid. Guess he won't be payin'
'em now, either."

"No," Rhodes said. "He won't. Did Ruth fill you in?"

"Sure did. You had a busy night."

Lawton stopped sweeping and leaned on his broom.
Rhodes knew this was a bad sign. It meant that the two men
were ready to talk and that they knew something he didn't
know.

That was bad because it would take forever for him to get it out of them, whereas he was ready to continue his investigation of Graham's death. He wanted to go back to Obert, talk to the people who lived around the college. He wanted to get in touch with the people whose numbers had been in Graham's wallet, Wallace and Rolingson, to see what they knew about the death, if anything. He needed to look inside Graham's house, try to find a key for the door to which the rope had been tied, and see what was behind that door. He wanted to talk to Brame again, too, but all that would have to wait until he heard whatever it was that Hack and Lawton had to tell.

"Any other calls last night?" he said to get the ball rolling.

"Nope," Hack said. "Nothin' out of the ordinary, that is. One little wreck. One break-in. Buddy got to the break-in and scared some kids off. Didn't catch 'em, though. He got there before they took anything."

There was nothing unusual in those items. Rhodes began to relax a little.

"How about this morning?" he said. It was a little early for anything to have happened, or so he hoped.

"Just one call," Lawton said.

Hack looked over at him. As the dispatcher, Hack took the calls, and he felt he had a right to get the story started.

Rhodes sat at his desk and started thumbing through his paperwork. He picked up Brame's card, still lying there, and put it into his shirt pocket. Then he turned around and waited. He was going to hear the story, but it wasn't going to be straightforward. It hardly ever was.

Hack and Lawton were looking at him expectantly.

"Well?" he said.

"Fran Newly called," Hack said. "From the Covered Wagon."

The Covered Wagon was a restaurant on the south side of town, locally famous for its family-style meals, which as far as Rhodes could determine meant that everything they served was fried, except for the breakfast biscuits, which weighed in the vicinity of a pound each. Rhodes had eaten there several times, but not recently. The risk of heartburn was too great.

Fran Newly, the owner, was a colorful character. She was a widow, about sixty, and she ate all her meals at the Covered Wagon. As a result she weighed in the neighborhood of two hundred and thirty pounds. She liked to mingle with the customers, particularly the male customers, and joke with them while they ate. There were some who said that Fran was still a lusty woman, but Rhodes wouldn't know about that.

"What was Fran's problem?" Rhodes said.

"It was the trash," Lawton said, getting it in before Hack could say anything.

"What trash?"

"In her dumpster," Lawton said.

"It wasn't *in* the dumpster," Hack said, taking over. "Leastways, she didn't think it was."

"What was it?" Rhodes said. "A rat?"

Hack and Lawton laughed. "You might say that," Lawton told him. "A white rat." They laughed again.

Rhodes was getting impatient, but he controlled himself. If he let his restlessness show, they would just slow down. He might never find out what they had to tell him.

"So it was a rat," he said.

"Not exactly," Hack said. "Not unless rats wear clothes."

"It had on clothes?" Rhodes was getting confused.

"Not many," Lawton said. "Just shoes and socks."

"Shoes and socks?" For some reason Rhodes thought of Mickey Mouse.

Hack had decided things had gone on long enough. "Fran went out to dump some trash after the breakfast rush," he said. "Threw back the dumpster lid, and it made a hell of a racket. You know how that lid sounds when you bang it against the back of that big metal thing. Anyway, it must've woke up somebody who was sleepin' behind the dumpster, and he came out. Like to scared Fran to death."

Rhodes wouldn't have thought anything was apt to scare Fran, especially the kind of man who was likely to sleep behind a dumpster. He said so.

"This 'un scared her, all right," Lawton said. "The fella that came out was stiff-starch nekkid."

"Not nekkid," Hack said. "He had on his shoes and socks."

"Tennis shoes," Lawton said. "White socks."

"That's all?" Rhodes said.

"That's all."

"Can she identify him?"

Hack and Lawton started laughing so hard that Rhodes was afraid they might have strokes.

When they finally got their breath, Hack said, "Yeah, she can identify him. She said she wanted us to hold a lineup and let her pick him out."

Rhodes didn't see what was so funny about that.

Hack was only too glad to explain. "She said she wouldn't mind meetin' the fella again, but she didn't think she could identify his *face*. So we'd have to have a special kind of a lineup for her. She said she knew we sometimes used officers, just to check on whether folks was takin' the lineup seriously, and she thought it'd be nice if that cute Sheriff Rhodes was put in there just to keep her honest."

Hack managed to keep a straight face through his explanation, but Lawton was snorting through his nose and clinging so hard to the broom for support that Rhodes thought his knees must have gone out on him.

"I guess it would be all right with her if we put you two in there along with me," Rhodes said.

Lawton stopped laughing immediately. "Ain't no old woman gonna get a look at me like that," he said. "I ain't even got a pair of tennis shoes. Hack, he can do it. 'Cept Miz McGee wouldn't like it.''

Miz McGee was Hack's romantic interest. He didn't like her name being brought into the discussion.

"You better take that back," he said.

"Will not," Lawton said.

They might have gone on like that for quite some time, but someone came into the jail.

It was a man of about forty-five. He was wearing faded jeans and low-heeled boots that were caked with dried mud and cow manure around the soles, a faded brown Western shirt, and a stained Houston Oilers gimme cap. His face was weathered, and he hadn't shaved for two or three days.

"You the sheriff?" he said, looking at Rhodes.

"That's right," Rhodes said standing up. "What's the trouble?"

"Somebody stole my damn cows," the man said.

The man's name was Seth Adkins, and he had a little herd of cattle near the Milsby community. Or they had been there until four or five days ago.

"Ten of 'em," he said. "Pretty things. Six heifers and four little calves. Might be another calf or two by now. Those other heifers was springin'."

He didn't know when they'd been stolen. "I been out of town for more'n a week. My sister in Dallas had surgery on her gall bladder. Got nearly fifty rocks outta there, one of 'em big as a golf ball. Her husband's dead, and I had to go help with her kids while she was out of the house. I come back last night, and when I checked on the cows, they was gone."

There was another problem, too. The cattle were all un-registered. They represented a broad mixture of breeds, and they had not been branded.

"Too damn much work," Adkins said. "I can't afford a

squeeze chute, and one man can't hardly do the brandin' without one."

"It would have helped us find the cattle, though," Rhodes said. Brands had to be registered with the county clerk, and while they could be altered, it wasn't easy to do a clean job of it. If anyone tried to sell the cows at auction, they could be traced quickly to the thief. Branded cattle were also a lot easier to spot in a pasture.

"Well, I didn't brand 'em. Some of 'em got marked ears, though."

"Split?" Rhodes said. "Underbit? Overbit?"

"Split," Adkins said.

That meant that he had literally split the end of one ear rather than taking a chunk out of the top or bottom. Unfortunately, that was a common way of marking cattle, and it didn't prove a thing to find a cow marked that way.

"Any other distinguishing marks on any of them?" Rhodes said.

"One of 'em's got the left horn missin'," Adkins said. One's got a bad left front hoof."

That might help, but Rhodes didn't think it would help enough.

"How about plastic ear tags?" he said.

"Don't use 'em," Adkins said. "Brush pulls 'em out."

"I hope you're not counting on our finding them?"

"Somebody stole 'em. You're the sheriff. It's your job to find cattle thieves." Adkins said it in a determined way and set his jaw. It was clear that he expected Rhodes to find the cattle, and to find them quick.

"We'll do our best," Rhodes said.

When Adkins had left, Rhodes had Hack get in touch with Ruth on the radio.

"Tell her to meet Adkins at his pasture and see if she can find any trace of the thieves. I've got to talk to Brame about

Simon Graham. If any emergency calls come in, get Buddy to handle them."

"Right," Hack said. "What about that lineup?"

"We've got to find a suspect first," Rhodes said.

He knew that wasn't likely. The naked man had no doubt been someone who had drunk a little too much the night before. There were more than enough people like that in Blacklin County. He had then slept it off in a convenient spot, and he would be long gone by now. Fran had probably scared him as much as he had scared her. Maybe more. Rhodes wondered if she had tried to catch him.

Brame was staying in the Lakeway Inn. Rhodes parked in front of room 133, got out, and knocked on the door.

Brame opened the door. "Good morning, Sheriff," he said. "I was expecting you a little earlier."

"Some things came up," Rhodes said, looking around for a place to sit.

The room held only a dresser, a bed, and two uncomfortable-looking thin-cushioned chairs by a small table; on the table were the remains of Brame's room-service breakfast—a coffee cup and a plate with scraps of egg, a few crumbs of bacon, and about a spoonful of grits and butter. Rhodes thought of his own healthy bowl of cereal with regret. He would have preferred eggs and bacon. And grits and butter, lots of butter. Ivy was death on butter.

Brame walked over to the table and moved the plate over to the dresser. "We can sit here," he said.

Rhodes sat on one of the chairs, which proved to be just as uncomfortable as it had appeared.

"How well did you know Simon Graham?" Rhodes said when he had gotten settled.

"As well as most anyone, I suppose," Brame said. "I had occasional business dealings with him."

"Do you know someone named Marty Wallace?"

"Ah, the lovely Marty. Simon's 'friend,' I suppose we

should call her. Yes, I know Marty. They were very close, if you know what I mean."

Rhodes could hear the contempt in Brame's voice. "You didn't like her?"

"I didn't like Simon, for that matter, but at least he was a businessman. Marty is simply greedy."

"What about Mitch Rolingson?"

"Simon's partner? Yes, I know him. He was the gofer, but he might have been smarter than Simon. He was the one who located the books. Simon made all the deals, however. Will Mitch be coming here?" Brame didn't sound particularly eager to see him.

"I'm sure he'll be here," Rhodes said. Then he got to the important question. "Can you think of any reason why Simon Graham might want to kill himself?"

Brame didn't even have to think about it. "Several. He was in extreme financial trouble, for one thing. He'd overextended himself. Buying that college campus was just one example of his foolish monetary policies. He had warehouses full of books that had never been cataloged, much less sold. And I've heard from reliable sources that most of the books are practically worthless. He had invested a great deal in them, far more than most people in the business thought they were worth, and he would never have realized a profit on them; in fact, he was losing his shirt."

"Are you sure?" Rhodes said.

"The book business is as full of idle gossip as any other, Sheriff," Brame said. "Perhaps more than most. But I'm as sure as I can be without looking at Simon's accounts."

"What about gambling?"

Brame leaned back and smiled. "You've heard about that, have you? Well, I can say for certain that's true. I was at Louisiana Downs one afternoon when Simon lost nearly fifteen thousand dollars. And from what I've heard, that was one of his *good* days. He didn't do well in Las Vegas, either. He loved to play cards, but he wasn't any good at it. I'm sure he lost a great deal more than he ever won."

"But he said he had this book for you, the one that's worth a lot of money. This *Tamerlane.*"

Brame's face changed. The smile was replaced by a poker face that would have done the Cincinnati Kid proud.

"He didn't say he had it for me. He just said he had it, and that it was for sale. I was hoping to see it. That's all."

"Tell me about it," Rhodes said.

"It's the first book by Edgar Allan Poe," Brame said. "Though his name doesn't appear on the title page, which says simply 'Poems by a Bostonian.' It was published in 1827, and it's an extremely valuable American first edition. Fewer than twenty are known to exist. I don't know its value precisely; there hasn't been one on the market in quite some time. But it would be worth a great deal of money if it's genuine. A very great deal. If Simon did indeed have a copy, it would have gone a long way toward getting him out of a deep hole."

"Did Graham come up with rare items like that very often?"

"More than you might think, though usually not of *that* rarity. But Mitch Rolingson was quite good at locating rare and costly books and papers in places that no one else seemed to know existed."

"And all of them were authentic?"

Brame's face remained frozen. "I couldn't say about that, Sheriff. There have been rumors. But only rumors."

"Could a book like this *Tamerlane* come into Graham's possession without a big fuss? It seems to me that something like that would cause a stir if it went on the market. And that there might be more reliable customers than Simon Graham."

Brame smiled. "Very astute, Sheriff. If the book had been sold through normal channels, most likely at an auction, everyone would have known. That obviously wasn't the case."

"What other channels are there?" Rhodes said.

"He *might* have gotten the book through another dealer, though that isn't likely. The only real possibility is that he's had it for quite some time."

"Then why didn't he sell it before now?"

"Well," Brame said, "he might not have *known* he had it."

"I don't see why not," Rhodes said. "If a man had something as valuable as that, he'd know all about it. You said it was a famous book."

"It could simply have been stored away in one of those warehouses I mentioned," Brame said. "Mixed in with all the others, most of them worth next to nothing. He could have been going through the books, maybe even trying to catalog them, and stumbled across it. It would have been a very exciting find. Very exciting." Brame's eyes were alight, and he rubbed his small hands together, almost as excited as if he had found the book himself.

Rhodes stood up. "All right, Mr. Brame. I appreciate the information. You're free to go back to Houston whenever you want to. I hope you'll stay in touch with me, though. I might need to talk to you again."

"I'll be right here, Sheriff," Brame said. "I want to see that book, if Simon really had it."

"So do I," Rhodes said.

5

THERE WERE PLENTY OF BLUEBONNETS AND INDIAN PAINT-brushes to be seen in the bright morning sunshine as Rhodes rounded the curve that led into Obert. There were, however, only a few of the pink flowers that Rhodes had always called buttercups but that Ivy had informed him were primroses. They would come along later, and he would still call them buttercups in spite of Ivy's correction.

He came to the small town, drove past the post office and several deserted buildings, went directly to the house where Graham had been staying, and parked in front of the garage.

The front door of the house was not locked. It was likely that Graham had picked up the habits of his rural neighbors; no one in Obert worried very much about locking doors. Or they hadn't in the past. Graham's death might change that.

Rhodes entered the living room and looked around. Whatever else you could say about Graham, he had been a neat housekeeper. The hardwood floor was shiny, and there was no dust on the coffee table or the lamp table. There was a copy of the current issue of *Texas Monthly* on the coffee table. There was also a copy of the Sunday supplement that Ivy had told Rhodes about. Graham's picture was on the cover; he was wearing virtually the same getup Rhodes had seen on the hanged man.

Rhodes was glad he wouldn't have to visit the library. He picked up the magazine, folded it once, and put it in his back pocket.

In one of the house's two bedrooms there was a desk. On top there were a clean desk pad, a Smith-Corona portable electronic typewriter, and a beer stein that held three ball-point pens and one No. 2 yellow pencil.

The drawers of the desk were empty except for a few blank sheets of white typing paper. There were no keys that might have fit the door to which the rope had been tied. There were none in the equally clean, equally empty bedroom, either. It was almost as if Graham didn't live in the house at all, and Rhodes supposed that was the case. Graham lived in Houston; he visited Obert.

The kitchen provided no more information than the rest of the house. The refrigerator was better stocked than Rhodes's had been before his marriage, but that was all you could say for it. There were no delicacies, unless you counted the six-pack of Seagram's wine coolers with one bottle missing. The rest of the contents consisted of the staples. Milk, bread, eggs, cheese, sausage. Rhodes thought again, ruefully, about his breakfast and about how sausage smelled when it was sizzling in the pan. A couple of pounds of ground meat and what looked like a small roast wrapped in clear plastic were in the freezer.

Rhodes went back outside. There was a woman standing by his car.

"Heighdy, Sheriff," she said. She was about fifty-five years old and wore faded jeans and, in spite of the increasing heat, a moth-eaten high-school letter sweater with a big white "O" on a black background. She may have attended public school in Obert back in the days when it had a school. There was dirt under her fingernails. She had probably been working in flowerbeds or a garden, though Rhodes hadn't noticed her when he drove up.

"I'm Oma Coates," the woman said. "I live right over yonder." She pointed to a white-painted frame house across the graveled street, the only house that was near the college grounds. "I heard about Mr. Graham."

It would have surprised Rhodes if she hadn't. There had been a number of people crowded outside the main building the night before, curious neighbors who had been roused from their sleep by all the activity and the flashing lights. One of them could easily have been Oma Coates, and all of them would be talkative.

Red Rogers would be after Rhodes soon, he was sure.

"Good morning, Miz Coates," Rhodes said. He didn't have to say any more. She looked as if she had something that she wanted to tell him.

"It's got where it's not safe nowhere," she said. "It's got where there's trash no matter where you go."

Rhodes understood that by "trash" she didn't mean debris, but human beings who didn't meet her own high standards.

"Just like hogs," she said. "Worse. Hogs won't kill their own."

Rhodes nodded. That was all the encouragement Miz Coates needed.

"They say he mighta killed hisself, but he didn't. It was them Applebys done it," she said. "Trash, ever' one of 'em. I hope you're gonna arrest the whole shitaree."

"Who are the Applebys?" Rhodes said. The name was familiar, but he couldn't quite place it.

Miz Coates tilted her head sideways and looked at him. "And you the high sheriff of the whole county." She shook her head. "Uh-uh-uh."

"I'm sorry," Rhodes said. "But maybe if you told me about the Applebys I could do something about them."

"They live right down this road," Miz Coates said. "Less'n a mile. Live like hogs. Worse. Hogs're cleaner'n the Applebys."

Rhodes remembered then that there had been several complaints called in from Obert about three months previously, all of them about a new family that had moved into the community. That family was the Applebys. The complaints had been anonymous, but Rhodes had a feeling he knew now who had made the calls.

"What's wrong with the Applebys?" he said.

"They're outlaws, that's what's wrong," Miz Coates said. "And they live like hogs."

"Worse," Rhodes said before he could stop himself.

Miz Coates looked at him suspiciously, but Rhodes didn't look away.

"Well, they do," she said. "But they're outlaws, too. Things have gone missin' around here since they moved in, lots of things."

"What kinds of things?" Rhodes said.

"My lawnmower, for one. I got it out last week, first time this year. Had to go in to get me a drink of water after I got the front mowed, so I just left it out in the yard. When I come back, it was gone."

"And you think the Applebys took it."

"Know they did. They go to that flea market at Colton ever' month to sell stuff. Like lawnmowers."

"Is that all?"

"Cows. If I was you, I'd check their herd. Never the same size two weeks in a row, if you ask me. And I wouldn't be surprised if they didn't go in folks' houses. They prob'ly killed Mr. Graham, too, when he caught 'em prowlin' his buildin'."

"Did you see them in there last night?" Rhodes said.

Miz Coates hesitated, and Rhodes wondered why. He was pretty sure she was about to tell him something important. But she didn't.

"Nope," she said. "I didn't see 'em. All I seen last night was a black car parked over there. Looked like a box on wheels. But I seen them Applebys in there plenty of times, least I seen them twins, Clyde and Claude. They ain't but about sixteen, but they're mean 'uns."

"Did you see any lights in the buildings last night?" Rhodes said.

"No sir, no lights. Them Applebys don't need no lights. They can move in the dark like a ghost."

Rhodes thought it would be a good idea to look in on the Applebys as soon as he had spent a little more time in the main building.

"What about a crew working over there?" he said. "I know Mr. Graham was planning to restore the whole campus, make a museum of it. Did he have workmen over there a lot?"

"Not since he got that house fixed up," Miz Coates said. "That was the first thing they did, and the last one. That Mr. Graham talked big, and mostly folks around here believed him. At first they did, anyhow. But then all the work stopped, and we knew he was never really gonna do what he said. He was just blowing a lot of hot air."

Rhodes thanked Miz Coates for her information and promised to make a thorough investigation of the entire Appleby clan that very day.

She went on back to her yard, but Rhodes was pretty sure she was not completely satisfied with either his promise or his abilities. He saw her shaking her head as she went and muttering "Uh-uh-uh" to herself.

He had met a lot of people like her in the course of his career. She lived alone and had a lot of time on her hands. She knew everybody's business and didn't mind talking about it. She probably kept a close eye on everything that went on in the vicinity, and Rhodes was sure she had seen more at the main building than she had told him about. He wondered what it could have been.

Rhodes went on around to the front of the old building. Ruth had strung a strip of the stretchy yellow plastic ribbon across the columns. The black lettering on the ribbon warned the public not to cross the police line.

Rhodes ducked under the plastic and entered the building. Light slanted in through the long windows with their irregular glass panes. Rhodes wondered how old the glass was. Probably as old as the building itself, he thought. The paint on the window frames was crackled and peeling, the putty was falling out, and there was a musty smell in the air that Rhodes had not noticed the night before. He supposed the heat caused it.

He mounted the stairs. The third floor was exactly as it had been left, with one exception. The door to which the rope had been tied was open.

The room itself looked even more of a mess in the daylight than it had in the dark. Someone had made a half-hearted attempt to paint the rear wall, but since there were about six earlier coats of paint that had not been cleaned off, the attempt had made things worse rather than better. The floor was dirty, and there were little piles of dirt in the corners. Cobwebs were thick in the rafters above, and Rhodes watched as one broke off and drifted slowly down to the floor. Why Graham had done anything at all to the room was a mystery to Rhodes, since what had been done was worse than nothing.

He crossed the wide room, though he could see even from where he was that there was no sign that the door had been forced. He did not try the knob; he would let Ruth Grady dust it for prints again, though he didn't really put much stock in fingerprints. He thought they were highly overrated as evidence.

Behind the open door was a small one-window room that had apparently been Graham's real office. There was a desk in there, and there were papers on it. There was a six-foot bookshelf, and there were several books on the shelves.

Most of them appeared to be about book collecting. None of them looked very old or valuable to Rhodes, but he was no judge.

He looked through the window. He could see for miles across the valley on the side of the hill opposite the one he'd come up. Several stock tanks were silvered by the sun, and he wondered if they were stocked with bass. April was coming up, and April was a prime bass fishing month.

Just then he heard a noise behind him. He turned in time to see two men jump up from behind a pile of lumber and run toward a window opening.

"Stop!" Rhodes yelled, but neither man—or boy, for they were no more than teenagers—paid any attention to him. They dived through the window.

There was no danger in that. The window opened into a large metal tube that Rhodes knew was the fire escape. There had been one just like it in the elementary school he had attended. Everyone had loved fire drills because the tube contained a circular slide leading to the ground. It was the next best thing to going to the park. Maybe it was even better, since the tube was almost completely dark inside.

Feeling like an awkward fool, Rhodes ran to the fire escape and climbed in. He hoped he didn't get stuck and thought fleetingly that if he escaped this time, he would definitely ride the stationary bike more often.

The slide was quite slick, and Rhodes was convinced that this was not the first time the two young men had used it. He twisted rapidly to the bottom of the chute.

When he shot out the opening at the bottom of the tube, his feet hit the ground and he tried to take off at a run. He'd always been able to do that when he was six or seven years old.

That had been a long time ago, however, longer than he liked to think about, and he wasn't quite as well coordinated as he had once been. He stumbled awkwardly for ten yards or so, his arms flailing as he tried to get his balance, and then stopped. He could see the boys fleeing across a pasture, and they were already so far ahead of him that he had no chance of catching them. Maybe if he had been six or seven, he would have tried. As it was, he simply watched them run.

They were both towheaded, lean, and muscular, with large hands and feet that had slapped on the floor like rubber. He hadn't seen their faces very well, but he was sure that they looked very much alike. Clyde and Claude, no doubt about it. The Applebys were getting more interesting all the time.

He walked back around to the front of the building and up the stairs. This time he had to stand for a minute and catch his breath after he got to the third floor. It was a long way up, and it seemed even longer the second time.

Then he got his third surprise of the morning. There was someone standing in the office, looking through the books on the shelves, pulling them out and opening them carefully.

It was a woman, and she had her back to Rhodes. She was tall, nearly as tall as Rhodes, and she was wearing a tight black skirt and a silky red blouse. She had long blond hair that caught the light from the single window, done in the crimped style that had been popular for a while. Rhodes couldn't get used to it. He thought it looked like Elsa Lanchester's hair would have looked in *The Bride of Frankenstein,* if she'd let it down. The woman was so intent on what she was doing that she didn't hear Rhodes come up behind her.

"I guess you don't believe in signs," Rhodes said.

The woman jumped and said, "Oh." She put the book she was holding back on the shelf and turned to look at Rhodes.

He looked back. She was in her late twenties and one of the best-looking women he'd ever seen close up. She had a perfectly clear complexion and the kind of cheekbones models would die for, along with deep blue eyes, red lips, and perfect teeth. Only the hair was wrong.

"You must be the police," she said. Though Rhodes did not wear a uniform, he had his badge on his belt, and he did wear a gun some of the time. He was wearing it today, but it was out of sight.

"The sheriff," he said. "Dan Rhodes. You did see the ribbon?"

"I saw it," she said. "I didn't think it applied to me. I mean, I might be the owner of this place now."

"You must be Marty Wallace."

"That's right." She stuck out her hand. She had long red fingernails and a firm, dry grip that held on to Rhodes's hand a little longer than he felt comfortable with.

"I thought sheriffs were supposed to be old men who wore big cowboy hats and whose stomachs hung over their belts," she said. "I didn't think they were supposed to be cute."

Rhodes shifted uncomfortably and tried to hold in his own stomach, which he was sure covered his belt buckle. He never wore a hat.

"Even if you do own this building, you shouldn't have crossed the line," he said. "And you shouldn't be here going through these books."

Marty put on a pouty mouth. "But they're mine. I mean, I'm sure Simon left them to me in his will. Why can't I look at them?"

"You can, if he did leave them to you, but not now. Right now, there's an investigation in progress."

Marty Wallace perched herself on the edge of the desk. Her skirt hiked up, and Rhodes looked at her eyes.

"The call I got last night didn't say what had happened," she said. "Was it an accident?"

Rhodes told her about finding Graham's body. Marty Wallace's eyes widened, and she gasped in horror.

"How awful!" she said. "I just can't believe Simon would kill himself!"

"He might not have killed himself," Rhodes said. "That's one of the things we're investigating. We didn't find a note last night, and I haven't been able to find one today. I thought there might be one in here."

Marty's eyes widened. "You're saying he was *murdered?*"

"It's a possibility."

Marty shook her head. "I don't believe it."

"Why not?" Rhodes said. "Just how closely were you and he associated?"

"And what exactly is *that* supposed to mean?" she said.

"Whatever you want it to mean. You said that you presumed that you were his heir."

"Oh. Well, yes, we were close. But you have to understand that we were nothing more than business associates."

"You're a rare book dealer?" Rhodes couldn't keep the surprise out of his voice. He knew it was a mistake to make assumptions about anyone based on appearances, but somehow he couldn't see Marty Wallace spending her time poring over the cracked leather spines of old books in some warehouse or store all day.

"I didn't say that. I was more like Simon's social director."

Rhodes remembered the parties Ivy had told him about. He felt his back pocket to make sure the magazine hadn't fallen out in the fire escape. It hadn't.

"I see," Rhodes said. Maybe she was telling the truth. That would explain her relatively calm acceptance of Simon's death. "I don't suppose you found a note of any kind in the desk drawers."

Marty shook her head, causing her blond hair to fall across her face. She brushed it back.

"No," she said.

The fact that she had not been authorized to look in the drawers seemed to bother her not at all. She had the kind of self-confidence that came from being the most beautiful girl in any crowd, the one that all the men wanted to please. Rhodes didn't think anything would bother her very much. She didn't even seem as bothered by Graham's death as Rhodes would have expected. Just the one little reaction, then calm again.

He changed the subject. "When did you get here, by the way? I didn't notice your car when I came."

"I just arrived," she said. "My car's parked right over by the house. I suppose that's your cruiser?"

"Yes," Rhodes said. "Do you have a key to this office?"

"No. Simon didn't let anyone in here. It was his inner sanctum. But the door was open, so I walked in. I do have a key to the house. I've stayed there a number of times. I hope I can stay there until all this is cleared up."

Rhodes thought about it. Did social directors get house keys? He didn't know, but he doubted it. However, he didn't see that it would do any harm for her to stay there now, and he said so.

"Good. I'll want to keep up with the progress of your investigation. If Simon was murdered—"

"I didn't say that. It's a possibility, of course."

"I still can't believe it. It's just too horrible."

"Do you think suicide is any better?" Rhodes said.

Marty pressed her lips together and drew the corners of her mouth down. "No. I don't suppose it is."

"Did Simon have financial problems? Gambling losses?"

Marty continued to frown. "You've been investigating, all right. Yes. It could have been those things. I suppose you know about the college, too."

Rhodes had to admit that he didn't.

"You might as well, then. Simon was six months behind on his note for this place. It was just a matter of time before he lost it, and if that happened, his whole life would have started unraveling."

"Why?"

"This would just have been the first thing to go. He wasn't meeting his other payments, either. He was paying the rent on his little shop in Houston, where he got his start, but that was all. He owed the rent for the warehouses where his books were stored. He even owed the caterers."

Rhodes thought about the ineptly painted wall. "Why was he working in here? His paint job is pretty bad, but he must have intended to do more. He had the scaffolding."

"He was trying to put up a front. The bank was insisting that the job show some progress. They didn't really want to call in the note, not the way things are now, and he was hoping to convince them that he really would be able to convert this place into a museum. The trouble was, he couldn't afford to hire a work crew."

Rhodes had not realized just how serious Graham's financial troubles were. Suicide now seemed more likely, but there was one thing Rhodes wanted to check. He had another question for Marty Wallace first, however.

"What about this book he was supposed to have, the one by Poe? *Tamerlane.*"

"He might not have had it," Marty said. "I never saw it. How did you know about that?"

"Someone told me. Is that what you were looking for here in the office?"

She actually blushed. "Yes. I thought it might be here. If it was, then it was mine, wasn't it?"

"Only if you're named the heir," Rhodes said. "I haven't heard about the will yet."

"It had better be mine," she said. Her face took on a hard look that made her only slightly less attractive.

"I'm sure it will be," Rhodes said. "But I'll have to ask you to leave now. I have a few more things to do up here."

"I wanted to get settled in the house, anyway," she said, moving past him and out into the large room. Her hips swayed to a rhythm that only she could hear. Rhodes tried not to watch. He told himself that he was a married man.

Somehow he didn't think that little fact would bother Marty Wallace one little bit.

6

WHEN MARTY WALLACE HAD GONE DOWN THE STAIRS, Rhodes went to the spot where Graham had been hanging. He looked at the scaffolding that lay on the floor where it had fallen over. Ruth had already checked it for prints, so Rhodes didn't mind touching it. He pushed it upright, and then began assembling the loose pieces.

It didn't take long to get it back together. When it was completed, Rhodes lifted up a board and put it across the top. Then he climbed up. It was a rickety and shaky structure; he didn't like climbing it, and he didn't like standing on the board when he got on top. Nevertheless, he stood there.

That was when he was certain that Simon Graham had not hanged himself, no matter what his various financial and personal problems might have been.

Someone else had killed Graham.

Even standing atop the scaffolding, Rhodes could not reach his hand as high as Graham's head had been. He couldn't reach it even standing on his toes and stretching as far as he could. It was still a foot or so out of his reach.

There was no way that Graham could have climbed up

there, slipped the noose over his head, and kicked the scaffolding out from under himself. Not considering where his head had been. Someone else had given him a lot of help.

More than he'd wanted, probably.

Rhodes climbed back down. He hadn't proved anything scientifically, but he was convinced. Someone besides Graham had hurriedly set up the scaffolding, not bothering to measure distances, in order to give the impression that Simon Graham had committed suicide. Which he hadn't. Rhodes disassembled the scaffolding and stacked it neatly.

"Are you the sheriff?" a man's voice said from behind him just as he finished.

Rhodes turned around. This place was getting as busy as an interstate highway. Ruth might as well never have put up the police line ribbon.

"I'm Sheriff Rhodes," he said. "Didn't you see the ribbon on the porch?"

The man was big, taller than Rhodes and much thicker from the neck down. He wasn't fat, either. His knit shirt stretched across his chest and bulged over his biceps; he looked as if he'd had the complete Charles Atlas course. He had a short blond brush cut, and Rhodes wondered if he liked Arnold Schwarzenegger movies.

For the second time that morning, Rhodes found himself sucking in his stomach and wishing he could keep himself on some kind of exercise program.

"I'm Mitch Rolingson, Simon's partner," the man said. He didn't look any more like a rare book dealer than Marty Wallace had. "I didn't think the police line applied to me."

Rhodes wondered what the world was coming to. Apparently no one thought anything applied to them if it told them not to do something they wanted to do.

He could almost understand Claude and Clyde's lack of compliance. From what Miz Coates had said, their family situation wasn't the kind to encourage obedience to the law.

But Mitch Rolingson and Marty Wallace should have known better.

"Did you happen to see Miss Wallace on your way up here?" Rhodes said.

"Sure did. She was the one who said it would be all right to come on up."

Rhodes nodded. Naturally. Why not? "She say anything else?"

"Not much. Just that you're investigating Simon's death. She says you think it could be murder."

"It could be," Rhodes said.

No one seemed to care much, one way or the other, whether Graham had been murdered or committed suicide, though. Neither Marty Wallace, Graham's special friend, nor Rolingson, his partner.

"It can happen anywhere," Rhodes said. No one seemed to care very much that Simon was dead or to mourn his passing.

"Could I get into the office?" Rolingson said, looking past Rhodes at the open door.

"Not right now," Rhodes told him. "I want to ask you a few questions, though."

Rolingson shrugged. "Go ahead."

"I understand that you were the one who located a lot of the books that Graham sold. Did you know that any of them were forgeries?"

Rolingson's face darkened and he clenched his fists. "Are you making some kind of accusation?"

"No. Just asking a question." Rhodes pulled the magazine out of his back pocket and showed it to Rolingson. "It's just something that I read about in here."

"That damned article," Rolingson said. "It's caused a lot of trouble, and it's all lies. Most of it, anyway. It should've been published in one of those scandal rags you buy in supermarket checkout lines."

"They must have gotten their information somewhere,"

Rhodes said. "This is a little more solid than something about a tribe of Eddie Cantor look-alikes being discovered in Brazil."

Rolingson snorted. "Not by much."

"But enough so that a big-city newspaper published it. They wouldn't do that without the legal department giving it a thorough going-over."

"Okay, maybe so. There was a little trouble one time with a forgery, but that wasn't my fault. Simon was the one who found the letters, not me."

"What letters?"

"The ones in the article. Those Byron letters."

"It wasn't a book?"

"Hell, no, it wasn't a book." Rolingson gave Rhodes a suspicious look. "I thought you said you read the article."

"I skimmed it," Rhodes said. If people could cross his police line without thinking about it, he could lie to them with a clear conscience.

"Well, it was letters. Nobody tries to forge books any-more. Old Thomas Wise did it pretty well, but he was about the last one, and that was a long time ago. Be a lot harder to get away with something like that these days. And damned if his forgeries aren't worth pretty good money now, if you could get your hands on one."

Rhodes looked over at the pile of lumber where Claude and Clyde had been hiding. He was tired of standing. "Come on," he said. "Let's sit down over there."

Rolingson followed him over and they sat. The room was getting much hotter as the sun kept streaming in through the glass of all the windows. Only a couple of the panes were missing, not enough to give any effective cross ventilation. There was a film of perspiration on Rolingson's forehead.

"Tell me about the letters," Rhodes said.

"I don't know where Simon got them. Byron letters aren't all that uncommon, you know."

Rhodes didn't know, but he nodded.

"What made these different was that they were to Byron's wife, Annabella Milbanke, after their divorce. They made explicit some things about Byron's relationship with his half sister, Augusta, that everybody already knew about but that no one had really been able to prove before. These letters proved it. They boasted about it."

Rhodes remembered Byron from high school. He could even have quoted a couple of lines from "So We'll Go No More a-Roving" if Rolingson had asked him, which didn't seem likely. But he didn't remember anything at all about anyone named Augusta. From the way things sounded, Byron's relationship with his half sister was not exactly the kind of thing that high-school teachers would have mentioned in Rhodes's day.

"I suppose that made the letters especially valuable," he said.

"Of course it did. They created a big stir; they were going to be the basis for a scholarly book. Simon got a shit-pot of money for them."

"Too bad they turned out to be forgeries," Rhodes said.

"Damned right," Rolingson said, pushing his right fist into his left palm and making the muscles of both arms bulge alarmingly. "If he hadn't had to pay back the money he got for those letters, Simon wouldn't have been in such bad shape."

"He had to pay back the money?"

Rolingson looked at Rhodes. "You really skimmed that article fast, didn't you? Yeah, he had to pay it back. The University of Texas didn't want any more forgeries."

"Any more?"

"Yeah, they've got most of Wise's. Anyway, the bad part was that they didn't catch on right at first that the letters were forged. Wise they knew about, but not this deal. Somebody had done a hell of a job, and the UT people *wanted* to believe in the letters. It took a while, and even at that they might never have suspected if someone hadn't put a bee in their bonnet. By that time, Simon had spent a lot of the money they paid him. He had to use everything he had and borrow a lot more to pay them back."

"Couldn't he have put them off?"

"If he'd done that, they'd have ruined him. When you deal in rarities, you've got to be completely above suspicion if you ever want to sell another book. Any hesitation, and Simon would've been dead."

Rolingson paused and looked up at the rafters. "Excuse my poor choice of words. Is this where he did it?"

Something about Rolingson's look bothered Rhodes. "It's where someone did it," Rhodes said. "What about this *Tamerlane?* Did you find that for him?"

"No. That is, I might have. It could have been in a lot I bought at auction, but I haven't ever seen it. I'd love to, though." Rolingson's eyes strayed again to the open door in the back wall.

"What about Hal Brame?" Rhodes said.

"That butthole. What's he got to do with anything?"

"He's here," Rhodes said. "He was going to look at that book, *Tamerlane*. Maybe he was going to buy it, if it was genuine."

"The hell he was." Rolingson's face darkened the way it had when Rhodes had mentioned the forgeries.

"Well, he didn't exactly say he was going to buy it. Just that it was for sale and that he wanted to see it."

Rolingson's face slowly returned to normal. "Maybe. I'm not even sure Simon would let that little worm look at it."

"Why not?"

"Who do you think hinted to the university that those Byron letters were forged?" Rolingson said.

Rolingson didn't have much more to tell. He said that he would be staying in Clearview if Rhodes needed him, and then he left. Rhodes watched him cross the room with his athlete's walk and went back to his inspection of the office.

He didn't find any more than he had found earlier, except that he understood more about at least one of the books on the shelves. It was a collection of the letters of Thomas J. Wise, and there were several volumes of Byron's letters as well. Rhodes wasn't interested in reading the no-longer-private correspondence of the two long-dead men, however. He had been hoping to find a copy of *Tamerlane,* but he should have known that he wouldn't. The open door pretty much assured that something as valuable as that would be gone, unless, of course, it had been very well hidden.

He wondered how many people in Blacklin County would have known its value. He could think of only three, none of whom was a resident, and one of them was at the Lakeway Inn, although that didn't mean he couldn't have visited the college earlier.

Rhodes decided that there wasn't much more he could learn in the old building. He had never put a lot of stock in clues, anyhow, for the same reason that he didn't think as highly of the computer as Hack did. Rhodes relied more on talking to people, trying to separate the lies from the truth, and trusting his instincts.

Before he went down the stairs, he walked over to one of the tall windows and looked out over the pasture that Claude and Clyde had been crossing when they ran away. There were cattle grazing in the pasture, and all around them there were the white birds that had suddenly appeared in the county some years ago. Cattle egrets, people called them. They lived off the insects that the cattle stirred up in their meanderings over the pasture, and there were always a great number of them around any herd.

Over near the barbed-wire fence by the road there were several cows standing together, well away from the others. Ten of them, by Rhodes's count. That was interesting, he thought.

It was time to pay a visit to the Applebys.

* * *

The gravel road that wound down the hill and past the Appleby place was lined with trees that grew at the edge of the bar ditches, and their limbs practically touched the sides of the county car. Or they would have, had it not been for one of the county's new purchases.

Rhodes referred to it as the tree-whacker, and the county commissioners were quite proud of it. It was a larger version of a power lawnmower, and the blades could be used to cut low brush or lifted and turned at a ninety-degree angle to chop the limbs off the trees growing by the road.

Rhodes was of the opinion that if there was enough traffic, the tree limbs would never get out over the road in the first place. The cars would keep them back.

The county fathers didn't see it that way. Or maybe they were just enamored of a new gadget. At any rate, they had bought the tree-whacker, and someone had been using it here. Rhodes could see the results, which were pretty much what you would expect. Tree limbs had been splintered and split, whacked off, and the clean wood showed like white, broken bones all along the road.

When Rhodes had discussed the tree-whacker with Hack, the dispatcher had been all in favor of it. "Them trees won't look so bad once they leaf out," he said.

Maybe. But right now they looked wounded, not to mention lopsided. The crew had not been along to pick up the mangled limbs, either, and they lay in the ditches, their few leaves withering and turning brown.

Rhodes parked by one of the ditches and got out of the car. The Easter spell had brought with it several inches of rain two days before, and the ground was still soft and muddy, especially in the bottom of the ditch. Rhodes's feet sank in as he pushed through the limbs and crossed the ditch to the fence. He carefully avoided the water in the ditch bottom.

The cows he had seen from the window were standing nearby. He counted ten of them, six heifers and four calves, two of the heifers heavily springing. One of the heifers was missing her left horn, and all of them had split ears.

There was nothing uncommon in that, but the fact that these cows were keeping themselves apart from the others in the pasture was unusual. Unless they were strangers to the herd, that is. That would make their standoffishness understandable. That, along with Oma Coates's assurance that the Applebys were outlaws, was enough to convince Rhodes that he should have Adkins come out and take a look.

He returned to his car and drove on to the Appleby house. It sat at the rear of a muddy lot that looked as if it had been trampled by a thousand hooves. The thick black mud was churned together with filthy hay, and there were wisps of baling twine mashed in as well.

A long gray cattle trailer stood off to one side, near a dilapidated barn. The sides of the trailer looked to be made of thin iron pipe and bands of aluminum. It was the most expensive thing in the yard.

Scrawny reddish chickens pecked in the mud around the barn. Rhodes hated to think what they might be finding to eat in the thick goo, and suddenly his cereal breakfast didn't seem so bad after all.

There was a fence around the lot, but the wooden gate sagged open. There was a wooden sign nailed to the gate. Faded letters, handpainted in red, said that there were HORSES AND COWS FOR SALE. Rhodes didn't see any horses, however.

The house was shaded by two large hackberry trees and looked as if it had not been painted since about the time of the Hoover administration. Its roof drooped, and there were a lot of missing shingles. One of the windows had no screen, but someone had nailed hardware cloth across the opening.

At that the house looked better than the barn. Its corrugated metal sides were streaked with rust, and they were peeling down from the top. Most of the roof was missing entirely.

Rhodes stopped the county car in the gateway. He didn't want to risk driving in the lot. He was afraid the car might sink in and never be seen again.

There was a girl standing on the porch of the house watching him. She wore a shirt that was about two sizes too small, a pair of faded cutoff jeans, and rubber thong sandals. Rhodes was instantly reminded of the cover painting of a book he had seen in Ballinger's paperback collection. *Backwoods Hussy.*

He got out of the car. He could smell mud, soured hay, and manure. "Is Mr. Appleby at home?" he said.

The girl shook her head. "He went into town."

Rhodes waited a minute, but the girl didn't have any more to say. "Are you Mrs. Appleby?" he said.

The girl gave Rhodes a look that wasn't exactly a smile. He would have called it a smirk if he had been sure exactly what that was.

"Mama's not feelin' so hot today," she said. "I'm Twyla Faye."

Rhodes waited again. The girl looked at him. Finally he said, "I'd like to talk to Claude and Clyde a minute."

The girl turned to the house and yelled through the screen door. "Hey, hotshots, the high sheriff here says he wants to talk to you."

She turned back and looked steadily at Rhodes. He waited, watching the screen door. It appeared that nothing happened very fast at the Appleby place.

After about three minutes that seemed a lot longer, the two boys came out. The screen slammed shut behind them. They stood hulking on either side of Twyla Faye, who Rhodes assumed must be their sister. Her hair was darker, but they all had the same moon-shaped faces, the same blue eyes that were as faded as Twyla Faye's jeans. All three of them looked at Rhodes vacantly.

"I saw you boys over at the college building a while ago," he said.

The twins didn't say anything. They just kept on looking at him. Their large hands dangled at the ends of long arms. Rhodes was beginning to wonder if the whole bunch was crazy. Or maybe they just couldn't hear him. He didn't relish the idea of walking across the yard.

"You were up on the third floor," he said, speaking louder. "You slid down the fire escape and ran back here."

"You can't prove nothin' on us," one of the boys said. Claude, maybe, or else Clyde.

"I'm not trying to prove anything right now," he said. "I just wondered what you were doing over there."

"We work for Mr. Graham," the other boy said. "Paintin' and fixin' up and all like that."

Rhodes couldn't say much for the quality of their work. "You were painting the third floor?"

"That's right," the boy said. "He was payin' us good money."

The girl laughed. "Ten dollars a day. They ain't too bright, Sheriff."

He wasn't sure how bright the girl was, either, but he suspected they were all considerably smarter than they were trying to appear. It wasn't unusual for people to play dumb when they were talking to the law, especially if the people didn't have too high an opinion of the law to begin with.

"A man died up there last night," he said.

There was no surprise on their faces. He hadn't expected any.

"We didn't have nothin' to do with that," Claude said. Or Clyde. "We don't know nothin' about it."

"You didn't see anyone up there last night? Any strangers?"

Claude and Clyde looked at each other. "We 'uz watchin' TV last night. We didn't see nothin' else."

It was becoming quite clear that the Appleby family

didn't reveal anything to the law, not in the way of normal conversation at any rate, and Rhodes didn't want to have to take anyone to jail, not just now.

"Nice looking herd of cows," he said, glancing back up the road.

The three on the porch looked casually in that direction, too. Then they turned slowly back to Rhodes.

"Yeah," Claude or Clyde said.

"When your daddy gets back from town, you tell him I dropped by," Rhodes said. "Tell him he can come by the jail and talk to me about those cows."

"What about 'em?" Twyla Faye said. The vacant look had left her face. She seemed almost interested.

"He'll know," Rhodes said. This time he didn't wait for an answer. He got into the car, backed out of the gateway, and drove back toward Obert.

On the way, he passed by the college again and looked toward Graham's house. There were two cars parked there, as there had been when he left, a white Chrysler LeBaron, which he assumed to be Marty Wallace's, and a dark green BMW, which he thought probably belonged to Rolingson. It just seemed like the kind of car Rolingson would drive.

But what Rhodes wondered about was why Rolingson had not gone into town as he had said he would. Was it possible that he wouldn't be staying at a motel after all? It was interesting to consider the possibilities, especially when you took into consideration the way Marty Wallace looked. And the fact that neither she nor Rolingson had so far shown the least sign of sorrow regarding Graham's death.

Both of them had surely wanted into that office, though, and Rhodes would not have been surprised if both of them weren't up there right that second, going over the bookshelf with a fine-tooth comb.

If they were, and he really didn't care, he just hoped they wouldn't find anything more than he had.

7

RUTH GRADY HAD FINISHED HER EXAMINATION OF ADKINS'S property by the time that Rhodes got back to the jail, and she was talking about it to Hack and Lawton. Rhodes looked on his desk for Dr. White's report of his findings on Graham's death. It was sitting on top of all the other papers, and he glanced at it quickly. There was nothing new in it, as far as he could tell, so he stepped over to listen to what Ruth had to say.

It turned out that there were no tire tracks at Adkins's gate because the rain from the Easter spell had effectively removed them. However, the grass was still mashed down where the thieves' trailer had been driven into the pasture for loading the cattle.

"I think I might have a lead for you," Rhodes said. "Why don't you get in touch with Mr. Adkins and take him out to the Appleby place." He told her where it was. "There are six cows and four calves bunched up by the fence, right by the road. One of the cows is missing a left horn. Let Adkins have a look at them, see what he thinks."

Hack looked impressed. "That's pretty slick detective work, findin' those cattle so fast," he said. "I guess you've solved the killin', too."

"Not yet," Rhodes said. He told them about his morning and that Graham's death had indeed been a "killin'."

"I bet it was the Applebys that did him in," Hack said. "I'm gonna check their criminal histories."

"While you're at it, check Rolingson, Wallace, and Brame," Rhodes said.

Hack grinned. "Right!"

"You've made an old man happy," Lawton said. "He's been itchin' to do somethin' like that all day."

"Do you really think the Applebys are involved in murder?" Ruth said.

"Maybe, maybe not. I don't know enough about them yet, and I wouldn't want to guess. Those two boys could be tough customers if they wanted to, though. They're big enough. I haven't met the father or the mother yet."

He was about to explain why when the door opened and Lamont Stanley, a thin man with thick glasses and graying hair, came in. He was the librarian at the Clearview Carnegie Library, and he was carrying a paperback book.

"Sheriff Rhodes, I want to report a crime," he said, ignoring the others in the office.

"What crime?" Rhodes said.

"Censorship!" Lamont said, his voice rising. "Censorship of the worst kind!"

"That's not exactly a crime," Rhodes said.

"If it isn't, I don't know what is," Stanley said. "It's an infringement of First Amendment rights, isn't it?"

"It could be," Rhodes said. "It depends."

"The First Amendment is part of the Constitution, isn't it?" Stanley was waving the book over his head now, as if it were a flag.

Rhodes admitted that it was.

Hack was paying no attention to the hubbub; his printer had started to chatter. Ruth went to stand by Lawton, and they were watching Stanley with amusement.

"And the Constitution is the Law of the Land, isn't it?" Stanley said.

Rhodes admitted that, too.

"Well, then," Stanley said, satisfied that he had made his point. "I want an arrest immediately!"

"Is that the evidence?" Rhodes said, indicating the book that Stanley continued to wave.

Stanley looked down at his hand in surprise, as if he had forgotten what he was holding. "Yes," he said, handing the book to Rhodes.

Rhodes took it and got out his glasses. The book was something called *Traces of Mercury,* by Clark Howard. On the cover was the head of a man who appeared to be wearing a hairnet. The man's head was flanked by the heads of a woman and another man. Beneath them were upside-down skulls. Pretty ominous stuff.

Rhodes opened the book and looked at the first page. He didn't see anything unusual about it.

"I'm afraid I don't quite understand the problem," he said.

"Just look," Stanley said. "Just look."

"I'm looking," Rhodes said, peering at Stanley over the top rims of his glasses.

Stanley snatched the book from Rhodes's hand, flipped through the pages, and handed it back. "Look right there."

Rhodes looked. Stanley had opened the book to page fifty-four, where someone had used Liquid Paper to white out a word in a sentence near the bottom of the page. Rhodes read the sentence, which had a word whited out in the middle: " 'I know that, for sake,' Madrigal said."

"You see?" Stanley said. "You see?"

"Is that all?" Rhodes said, looking around at Ruth and Lawton for help. They didn't offer any. Hack's printer was still racketing along.

"All!" Stanley said. "All?" He grabbed the book again

and flipped more pages. "Look there! Page sixty-seven!" He thrust the book back at Rhodes.

Rhodes looked at the sentence Stanley indicated, one word of which had been obliterated:

"   ," Tay sighed."

"You see?" Stanley repeated. "You see?"

"I see," Rhodes said. "The whole book's this way?"

"The whole book. It's ruined, of course. Just ruined."

"But it's only a paperback," Rhodes said.

It was the wrong thing to say. "Only a paperback!" Stanley said. "And what difference does *that* make? It's still a *book,* Sheriff Rhodes, and one of the patrons has complained about its mutilation. What if the culprit gets his hands on Faulkner and Hemingway? Would that make things any worse?"

"Who is this culprit we're talking about?" Rhodes said. "Do you have a name for me?"

That calmed Stanley down somewhat. "Well, no, not actually. We don't keep records of who checks out the paperbacks. We just write down the number that they take and check to see that they bring back the same number."

"Where do you buy the paperbacks?" Rhodes said. "This one looks pretty old." He opened it to the copyright page. "Nineteen seventy-nine."

"They're donated to us, actually," Stanley said. "We don't buy them."

"Donated?" Rhodes said. "Then how do you know this one wasn't marked by the original owner? Do you go over each one as it comes in to the library to make sure it hasn't been written in or that no pages are missing?"

It was a few seconds before Stanley spoke again. Then he said, "No. Actually, we don't. Go over the books when we receive them, I mean."

"So this one might very well have arrived in the library already marked."

"Yes," Stanley said, drawing the word out. Then he thought of something else. "But even at that, it's still censorship! I want whoever did this arrested at once."

"Who donated the book?" Rhodes said.

"I don't know," Stanley said. "We don't keep up with things like that, actually."

"And you don't know who checked it out, except for the person who complained about it."

"That's true."

"Then who do you want me to arrest?" Rhodes said. "Actually."

"Well, whoever did it, of course."

"And who is that?"

"Why, how should I know?" Stanley was amazed at the question. He looked at Rhodes quizzically. "That's your job, isn't it?"

"All right," Rhodes said. "Here's the way we'll work it. You go through all your paperback books and remove all the ones that have been censored. Then keep a close watch on the rest. Look over them when they're returned. As soon as one comes in with words whited out, we'll know who to arrest."

"But that means a great deal of work for me and my staff," Stanley said. "We don't actually have time—"

"You want the culprit arrested, don't you?" Rhodes said.

"Of course I do, but—"

"Then you'll have to do the work," Rhodes said. "If you care about the First Amendment, that is."

"Of course I care, but—"

"Well, then," Rhodes said. He handed Stanley the book and returned his glasses to his pocket.

Stanley took the book. "We'll do it," he said. He threw his shoulders back, did an about-face, and marched out of the office.

"He will do it, too," Ruth said, walking back across the office.

"Maybe," Rhodes said. He didn't expect the case of the self-appointed censor to amount to anything. It was probably just a onetime example of some overzealous reader who happened to have some Liquid Paper at hand, something that was not likely to be repeated. Or so he hoped. He didn't know what he'd do if Stanley insisted that the Sheriff's Office set a watch on the homes of everyone who checked out a paperback book.

"Let's see what Hack's got for us on that printer," he said, and they all gathered around Hack's desk.

"Those three book folks are clean as a hound's tooth," Hack said. "Not countin' a few movin' violations."

"Things like that don't amount to much," Lawton said. "Could happen to anybody."

"I guess," Hack said, glancing up at Lawton. "Never happened to me, though."

"What about the Applebys?" Rhodes said.

"Well, now," Hack said. "The Applebys are a whole different case." He handed Rhodes the printout.

It was longer than Rhodes would have thought. The Applebys had been busy, in a lot of different places, or at least the father had. Cy Appleby, the father, had first been arrested at the age of eighteen, not counting any juvenile records that were closed to the computer, and he hadn't slowed down since. He'd been picked up for burglary of a habitation, theft of services, assault, attempted murder, and even once for selling bootleg liquor.

"Bet he made it himself," Hack said.

"No takers," Rhodes said.

Despite his wide range of alleged criminal activities, however, Appleby had served very little time in jail. Only one of the arrests had led to a conviction, and that had been the burglary charge. He'd served two years in the Texas Department of Corrections Ramsey I Unit and been released only eighteen months ago. Since that time, he'd kept his record spotless.

As juveniles, Claude and Clyde didn't have records, and neither did Twyla Faye. Their mother, Leona, had been picked up on several occasions for soliciting, but had never served time. The family had moved around quite a bit, too, having lived in Harris County, Bell County, Austin County, and Brown County before moving to Blacklin County.

"Nice folks," Lawton said. "Wonder why they decided to settle here?"

"Prob'ly hadn't heard about the quality of the law enforcement," Hack said. "We already got 'em for cattle theft. Murder's next."

"Don't get in a rush," Rhodes said. "We don't have them on anything. Even if Adkins can identify those cattle, we can't arrest anyone. It's his word against the Applebys' word. Remember, he didn't brand those cows."

"We'll get 'em some way," Hack said. "Ruth's on the case."

Ruth grinned. She knew as well as Rhodes what Hack's first reaction to her had been.

"Speaking of being on the case," she said, "I'd better see if I can get Adkins out there to have a look. Those might not even be his cows."

"Bet they are," Hack said.

"No takers," Rhodes said.

It was past noon, so Rhodes went home to see if there was any of the meat loaf left. Ivy wouldn't be there. She took her lunch to work and ate in the office. By doing so she was able to leave at four o'clock rather than five.

There was meat loaf in the refrigerator, wrapped in aluminum foil, so Rhodes made himself a cold meat-loaf sandwich with a slice of low-fat imitation cheese on oat bran bread spread with mustard and low-cholesterol Miracle Whip. He didn't go as lightly on the Miracle Whip as he would have had Ivy been there. He got a Dr Pepper from the refrigerator and sat at the table going over everything that he knew or suspected about Simon Graham's death.

The murder, and he was sure that it was murder, seemed to hinge on the book by Poe. Everyone wanted it, but would anyone have killed to get it? Rhodes didn't know much about book collecting, aside from his acquaintance with Ballinger, but it seemed that book collectors had a kind of intensity that might very well lead them to do some drastic things, maybe even kill someone.

The open office indicated that someone had gotten in with a key. Had the key been taken from Graham? If so, who took it? Brame was the only one who admitted to being anywhere near Obert when the crime was committed. Ruth had called Marty Wallace and Mitch Rolingson to inform them about Graham's death, and they had shown up. But he hadn't asked Ruth whether she actually reached them. She might have left a message on their machines. It seemed that everyone had an answering machine these days. He would have to check that with Ruth.

If they were not at home, they could easily have been in Obert. The fact that Miz Coates had not seen their cars didn't mean a thing. There were several places out of sight of her house where they could have been parked. He remembered Miz Coates's hesitation when he asked if she'd seen Claude or Clyde over at the college building the previous night. She had volunteered the information that she'd seen only one car, but he suspected that she had been holding something back. He'd have to talk to her again, too. It might be that she had seen the other cars but neglected to mention them because she'd seen them before and knew whom they belonged to.

And then there were the twins, along with their father and the rest of the family. They were certainly big enough to have killed Graham. But why would they want to?

Rhodes looked down at his plate. There was nothing left

of the sandwich but a few crumbs. He thought for a minute about going into the other room and riding on the stationary bike for a few minutes, but he thought that he recalled reading somewhere that it wasn't good to exercise so soon after eating. And even if that wasn't true, he didn't feel much like riding a bicycle anyway. He tried to put the thought of riding it out of his mind.

To distract himself, he went to the phone and called the jail to ask Hack if Ruth had come back in.

"You bet she has, and she has Mr. Adkins with her. He's hoppin' mad. You better get on back down here."

"What's the trouble?" Rhodes said.

"He says those are his cows, all right, and he wants 'em back right now. He's threatenin' to go out there and steal 'em back if we don't get 'em for him."

"I'll be right there," Rhodes said. He had been planning to stay at home a little longer, but to tell the truth he didn't mind at all that he had to return to the jail.

That way, he wouldn't feel guilty about not riding the bicycle.

8

WHEN RHODES GOT BACK TO THE JAIL, RUTH GRADY HAD succeeded in calming Adkins down somewhat, but his tight mouth was still fixed in a frown.

"I don't know what kind of a country it is," he said, "where a man can rustle your cows right out of your own pasture, and then when you find 'em, you can't do a thing about it."

"Are you really sure they're yours?" Rhodes said. "There's no mistake?"

"What do you think I am, some kinda damn idiot?" Adkins said. "I know my own cows when I see 'em."

"They knew him, too," Ruth said. "They came right to the fence when he called them."

Rhodes didn't know that people trained cows to come when called, and he admitted it.

"Well, I trained 'em," Adkins said. "I named 'em, too, ever' one of 'em. Millie, she's the one with the missin' horn. Lynette's her calf."

"And Sally was there too. She's the one with the bad hoof," Ruth said. "He's not kidding, Sheriff."

"So what're you gonna do?" Adkins said. "Now that you know they're mine."

Rhodes had to admit that he didn't quite know what to do. He told Adkins that he would drive back out to Obert and have a talk with Appleby, who of course had not shown up at the jail even though Rhodes had left the message that he wanted to talk to him.

Rhodes hadn't expected him to come, really, even if Twyla Faye and the twins had mentioned Rhodes's visit. They may have forgotten it, or they might have simply been in the habit of keeping their mouths shut. And there was always the possibility that someone like Appleby wouldn't visit the sheriff just because the sheriff wanted him to. Rhodes thought that possibility was the strongest of all.

"What do you think he's gonna do with my cows?" Adkins said. "He sure as hell won't just give 'em back to me. Next auction day, they'll be sold, sure as I'm standin' here. You gotta do somethin' about this."

Rhodes didn't know what Appleby intended to do with the cows, but it seemed likely he would eventually sell them at auction, as Adkins said.

"I'll do my best to get them back for you," Rhodes said. "It might take a while." He didn't have any good ideas about how to do what he was half promising. He didn't have any more right to take the cows than Adkins did.

"It better not take too long, whatever you do," Adkins said. "I'll go after 'em myself if it does."

"I don't think that would be a good idea," Ruth said. "The sheriff and I have seen the cattle on Appleby's property, and we can identify them." She looked over at the dispatcher. "And Mr. Jensen's heard you threaten to go after them. If you take them from Appleby, he can file charges on you and we'd all be the witnesses."

Adkins shook his head. "It's a hell of a note that something like this can happen to a man in the United States of America," he said. Then he brightened. "What if you asked him and he can't prove those cows and calves belong to him? What would happen then?"

"Then we'll have a little better chance of getting them back for you, based on your identification of them," Rhodes said. "But not much better. It's your word against his."

"A hell of a note," Adkins said.

Rhodes had to agree with him.

When Rhodes passed by the college, he noticed that the cars of both Marty Wallace and Mitch Rolingson were still parked by Graham's house. He had checked with Ruth and found out that she had spoken to neither of the two in person early that morning; she had left messages on their answering machines and asked them to call the Sheriff's Office. They had both called Hack within twenty minutes, and he had broken the news to them about Graham's death.

"Didn't tell 'em too much about it, though," Hack said. "Just that he was dead. They didn't seem too tore up about it, let me tell you."

That fit with their reactions when Rhodes had talked to them. They seemed a lot more interested in searching the office than in hearing about Graham's death. Rhodes wondered again just how much a book like *Tamerlane* might be worth.

The fact that the two of them had responded so quickly after Ruth's message might make it seem that they had been out late and called as soon as they had returned home, but Rhodes knew that wasn't necessarily so. They might have answering machines from which they could retrieve their messages simply by calling the machine and punching in a code on the phone they were using. Computers weren't the only electronic marvels these days.

In other words, they could have been in Obert just as easily as they could have been in Houston. There was no way of knowing for sure. Not yet, anyway. Later, if he had to, he could check their long distance records.

Ruth had developed plenty of prints from the third floor,

but even if some of them belonged to Wallace and Rolingson, they could say that they had been there any number of times prior to the night of Graham's death. It was almost a certainty that their prints weren't on file anyhow, so there wouldn't be any matching up unless Rhodes could obtain some prints to match them with. It was almost as frustrating to think about as the stolen cattle were.

Rhodes slowed down and looked over the campus. It would be easy to conceal a car behind the gymnasium or the dormitory if you didn't want anyone to know you were there. Even behind the main building. Wallace and Rolingson would have been there often enough to have known that.

He looked back at the road just in time to catch a movement out of the corner of his eye. He glanced in the direction of Miz Coates's house and thought he saw a curtain move slightly. He wasn't surprised. Miz Coates was obviously a woman who liked to keep up with everything that was going on in her general neighborhood. She had the only house on the opposite side of the road from the campus, and Rhodes suspected that she knew quite a bit more about the goings-on around there than she had told him. He would have to talk to her again soon.

But first he had to go to see the Applebys.

This time there was a pickup parked in the Applebys' yard when Rhodes got there. It was a bright red Chevrolet Silverado with an extended cab, and it looked as if it had just been washed and waxed. The silver hubcaps gleamed, and the shine on the paint looked six inches deep. The pickup must have cost much more than the house and barn were worth, and it had been driven into the yard very slowly and carefully so as not to get mud anywhere on it except for the tires.

There was no one in sight when Rhodes pulled the county

car up in the gateway, but by the time he had gotten out a man had appeared on the porch.

He was almost as big as Claude and Clyde, but not quite. His hair was much darker and longer than theirs, and there were streaks of gray in it. It curled out from beneath a sun-faded California Angels baseball cap and hung down his neck in the back. He was also wearing old jeans that were stuck into the tops of black, mud-caked boots. Rhodes thought the halo on the big *A* on the front of the cap was probably as close as Appleby would ever come to having one.

Appleby had a thick beard, streaked with gray like his hair, and he was chewing tobacco. It was hard to see his eyes, which were shaded by the bill of the cap, but Rhodes could see his arms where they came out the short sleeves of his plaid shirt. They were almost as big as Rolingson's. His hands looked as hard as if they had been sculpted from stone.

"You lookin' for me, Sheriff?" the man said.

"I am if you're Cy Appleby," Rhodes said, standing by his car. He still didn't relish the idea of walking across the muddy yard where the scrawny chickens continued to cluck around and peck for food, their heads bobbing up and down. Now and then one of them would stand still, head tilted up, and swallow.

"I'm Appleby," the man said. "What's it to you?"

"I want to ask you a few questions about your cattle," Rhodes said.

Appleby's lips curled into a hairy sneer. "Yeah, my kids told me you'd come snoopin' around here this mornin'. Too bad that you Laws can't never let a man live down his past mistakes. Let him serve a little time, and you're always on his case, one way or the other."

"I'm not on your case," Rhodes said. "It's just that we've had a report on some stolen cattle that happen to look a lot like some of the ones in your pasture."

"That's a funny thing about cows," Appleby said, leaning his wide shoulders against the porch wall and sticking his hands in the pockets of his faded jeans. "They all look pretty much alike."

Rhodes was no cattleman, and he agreed with Appleby. Adkins wouldn't have agreed, however. To anyone who knew cattle, they were as different and as individual as people, as Adkins's penchant for naming them proved.

"Still," Rhodes said, "it would be nice if you could prove ownership of your herd."

"Damn right, it would," Appleby said. "And I can. Least I can prove I own the ones you're worried about." He reached into his shirt pocket and brought out a folded paper.

"How do you know which ones I'm worried about?" Rhodes said.

"Hell, it's gotta be the new ones," Appleby said. "Anybody'd know that. The ones that kinda stay apart from the others till they get used to 'em."

"And I guess that paper's the auction receipt for them," Rhodes said.

"Damn right it is. I bought 'em a couple of weeks ago down at Colby." Appleby spit a brown stream of tobacco juice across the porch. It splatted on the mud.

Colby was the largest town in one of the adjoining counties, and there was a weekly auction held there. Rhodes didn't doubt that Appleby had a receipt. The trouble was that it was virtually worthless in one sense. Cattle auction receipts were notorious for their vagueness. "One whiteface heifer" would be a typical description. "Ring-eyed calf" would be another. Such descriptions could fit any one of dozens of animals.

"You wanta see it or not?" Appleby said.

"Yes," Rhodes said. "I'll look at it."

"Come right on over here and get it, then," Appleby said.

"Or are you afraid you'll get your shiny little kicks all muddied up?"

Rhodes looked down at his shoes, which weren't shiny at all. He didn't especially want to walk across the yard, that was true, but he would have done it if Appleby hadn't challenged him. Now he didn't intend to.

"Bring it to me," he said.

Appleby stepped away from the wall. "You gonna make me?" he said.

Rhodes sighed inwardly. He had met more men like Appleby than he liked to think about. They all thought they were tougher and smarter than anyone else, particularly if anyone else happened to represent the law. The fact that such men had been arrested numerous times, had even served time in prison as Appleby had, never seemed to have any effect on their confidence in their innate shrewdness. For them, every encounter was a challenge; every meeting was a confrontation. They never seemed to learn. Or care.

"I don't have to make you," Rhodes said. "I'm the sheriff."

Appleby thought about that for a minute. He spit again, and then he stepped off the porch, his boots sinking into the soft mud of the yard. He kicked at a chicken that was in his path, and it jumped out of the way, squawking and flapping. Appleby didn't even seem to notice. He walked slowly over to where Rhodes was standing. He stuck out the paper, and Rhodes took it, opened it, and smoothed the creases.

The receipt was just as vague as Rhodes had expected it would be. It might have been legitimate, probably was, but that didn't mean that Appleby couldn't have bought the same number of cattle that he had stolen. There was just no way to be certain. One thing was for sure, however. Appleby's receipt would look a lot better to a judge than anything Adkins could present.

Rhodes returned the receipt.

Appleby took it and stuck it back into his shirt pocket. "You satisfied?"

"For now," Rhodes said.

"Don't give me that 'for now' shit, Sheriff," Appleby said. "Those are my cows, and you can't prove no different. I don't know who told you they weren't mine, but I can guess." He looked up the hill toward the college. "I don't think he'll be tellin' anything else about anybody around there, though."

"You mean Simon Graham?" Rhodes said.

Appleby spit and wiped his mouth with the back of his hand. "Yeah, Graham, that sissy up on the hill. I guess somebody finally taught him to mind his own damn business. 'Bout damn time, too."

"It wasn't Graham," Rhodes said. He thought about standing on the third floor of the main building, looking out the window. Graham would have been able to see most of what went on in Appleby's pasture if he had wanted to.

"That meddlin' Coates bitch is the one, then," Appleby said. "It might be that somebody has to teach *her* a thing or two one of these days."

Rhodes shook his head. "Saying things like that isn't very smart, Appleby."

"Smart's ass. All I ask is to be let alone to take care of my cows, try to earn a honest livin'. But that's too much for some people. Always stickin' in their noses where they don't belong. They ought not to do that. They might get their noses cut right off."

"I take it you didn't think too much of Simon Graham, then."

Appleby spit and shifted his cud. "Fruitcake," he said.

"Your boys are working for him."

"I give him credit for that. Wouldn't nobody else around here hire 'em. But he was a snooper."

"Did you kill him?"

Appleby snorted, nearly losing his plug. "Hell, Sheriff, I

didn't know you were a comedian. Me? Kill somebody? You oughta know better than to ask me a thing like that. First you accuse me of stealin' cows, and then you ask me if I killed a fella. You must think I'm some kind of desperado." He pronounced the last word with a long *A*.

"I don't think anything, yet," Rhodes said. He got into his car, then leaned out the window. "Thanks for your cooperation," he said. He backed up and started up the hill.

He looked into the rearview mirror before he went around the first curve. Appleby was still standing right where Rhodes had left him, watching.

When Rhodes got back to the jail, the place was surrounded. Most of the cars, vans, and station wagons parked there had the call letters of various television stations painted on their sides. The one parked in Rhodes's own space was from the local radio station. Red Rogers. There were camera crews on the grass in front of the building, black cables slithering all around. The door of the building was open as reporters pressed forward, all trying to get inside at once.

It seemed as if the news of Graham's death had gotten around.

Rhodes parked across the street and got out of the car. He had been afraid of this, and now there was nothing for it but to go on over there and face up to them. It wasn't something he was looking forward to. He knew there were probably some sheriffs, somewhere, who actually enjoyed standing in front of a mini-cam and talking about their latest cases, but he certainly wasn't one of them.

The fact that he had never done it before didn't make thinking about it any easier. All the crimes in Blacklin County up to this point had been the kind that were of restricted interest. The death of Simon Graham was different, however. Graham was a man with a statewide reputation, a man the Sunday supplements commissioned articles about. His death was news. For now, anyway.

It wouldn't be news for long, Rhodes was sure. The furor would die down in a day or so. Graham hadn't been well-enough known to rate much more than one day of coverage. Maybe two if the news about *Tamerlane* leaked out. He wasn't going to be the one to leak it, however.

Since Rhodes didn't really look much like anyone's idea of a sheriff, not being in any kind of uniform, he didn't have too much trouble pushing his way through the mob and getting into his office. The trouble was that the place was so crowded that he couldn't get to his desk.

He had about decided to sneak back out to his car and go home to see what was on that afternoon's "Million Dollar Movie" when Red Rogers caught sight of him.

"There he is!" Rogers yelled. "There's the sheriff!"

There was confusion then, as cameras swiveled, reporters jumped, and everyone yelled and talked at once.

"Where?"

"Over there!"

"Which one?"

"Get outta the way!"

"Watch where you're going with that damn thing!"

Red Rogers, crouching low and slinging a wicked flurry of elbows, scooted through the tangle of cables, cameras, and reporters and got to Rhodes first. He shoved a microphone into Rhodes's face and said in his radio voice, "Sheriff Rhodes, please tell our tri-county listeners what you know about the Simon Graham case. Is it true that he was found hanging in the old Obert College main building late last night?"

By the time Rogers had finished asking the question, most of the cameras in the room were focused on Rhodes. Microphones bristled all around him. He looked beyond them at Hack and Lawton, who were sitting at the dispatcher's desk, watching with what looked like a measure of displeasure that they were not the ones being interviewed. They weren't going to be any help. Other reporters stuck their microphones at him, reaching over outthrust hands.

"Yes, that's true," Rhodes said. He couldn't think of anything to add, but that didn't matter. Red Rogers could think of plenty, and for now the other reporters seemed content to let him ask the questions.

"Was it murder, Sheriff? Or was it suicide?"

Rhodes looked around for Ruth Grady, but she was nowhere to be seen. He had to answer. "That hasn't been determined yet," he said, not exactly lying. He had determined to his own satisfaction that Graham had been murdered, but it hadn't been proved in a court of law.

"It is well known in book-dealing circles that Simon Graham was in financial difficulty," an icy blonde with lacquered hair said. "Do you think he took his own life in order to escape his debts?"

"I don't know that he *did* take his own life," Rhodes said.

The woman looked pleased. "Does that mean you think he was murdered?"

"I don't know about that," Rhodes said, wishing that he had never entered the building.

It went on like that for what seemed like a very long time, though it probably wasn't more than two or three minutes. It might have gone on longer, if Lamont Stanley hadn't come shoving through the door, dragging Miz McGee behind him.

"Sheriff, I want you to arrest this woman," he said.

There was more yelling, shoving, and general hullabaloo as the cameras shifted and the microphones got re-aimed.

"What's the charge?" someone called out.

Stanley looked at all the cameras with satisfaction. "Violation of the First Amendment!" he said.

9

IT TOOK A WHILE TO GET THINGS STRAIGHTENED OUT AFTER that.

Miz McGee, who was cold even in the warmth of spring, stood there looking as if she were dressed for an Arctic expedition, her upper body swathed in a thick black wool sweater, a red knit cap pulled down over her white hair. She seemed to have no idea at all about what was going on, and she stared around looking for Hack.

Hack, when he saw that Miz McGee was completely bewildered, came out of his chair and climbed over two cameramen and a reporter to get to her.

Stanley had his hand on Miz McGee's arm. Hack grabbed Stanley's hand and pulled it away, flinging it at the librarian and causing him to hit himself lightly in the face with his own hand.

"I'll make you think First Amendment," Hack said. "You leave Miz McGee alone."

Stanley made as if to take a swing at Hack, but there really wasn't room, and by that time Lawton had arrived. He grabbed Stanley's arm and twisted it up behind his back.

"You need to calm down," Lawton said, trying to back Stanley away from Miz McGee and Hack.

Rhodes was watching helplessly, hemmed in by all the bodies. No one was facing him now; all he could see were backs as everyone frantically tried to focus on the sudden and unexpected activity. No one knew what was going on, but that didn't stop them. After all, it might be news.

Rhodes opened the middle drawer of his desk and fished around inside until he found what he was looking for. He hadn't seen it for a long time, but he thought it would be there.

It was a silver-plated police whistle that someone had given him as a joke years ago. He had carried it on a chain for a few months, but never having had an opportunity to use it, he had tossed it into the drawer, where it had lain waiting for just this moment. The chain still hung from its silver-plated loop.

Rhodes put the whistle in his lips and blew.

The shrill blast pierced the hubbub in the office and created an instant of sudden silence.

"I want everyone from the news media out of here right now," Rhodes said. "We have some business to conduct."

There was a babble of noise. Rhodes picked out some words that sounded like, *"Now* who's violating the First Amendment?"

The words didn't bother him. He blew the whistle again.

"All of you are interfering with a Sheriff's Department investigation," he said when silence descended. "If there's a story here, you can have it later; but if you're not out of here in five minutes, I'm going to have to arrest every one of you."

The yammering started up again.

"He can't do that, can he?"

"I don't know, but he looks like he might try."

"We might go, but we're sure as hell coming back."

"Damn right."

Cameramen began backing out the door, mike cables slithered across the floor, reporters looked around for one last chance to ask a question and found no one willing to talk.

The office was cleared in less than the allotted time.

"Now," Rhodes put his whistle back in the drawer and turned to Stanley, "what's this all about?"

Lawton had released Stanley's arm, but he was still standing by the librarian and keeping a close eye on him. Stanley edged away from Lawton now that there was room to do so and glared at Miz McGee, whom Hack had taken to his desk and seated in his chair. She still did not seem to have any idea of exactly what was going on, but she was watching Stanley with bright eyes as if she wouldn't be surprised at anything he did.

"That woman is the guilty party," Stanley said. "She's the one who defaced the books."

"Is that right, Miz McGee?" Rhodes said.

"I don't know what he means," Miz McGee said. She looked up at Hack. "What's he talkin' about, Hack?"

"Maybe you'd better tell us the whole story, Mr. Stanley," Rhodes said.

It didn't take long. Miz McGee was a well-known library patron, being partial to the works of Barbara Cartland, most of which were available on the library's paperback racks rather than on the shelves of hardback books. Miz McGee regularly took home five or six of the Cartland novels, and when she had returned her most recent selection of books to the library that afternoon, Stanley's vigilance committee inspected them.

"And here's the evidence," Stanley said. He whipped a book from his back pocket and flourished it triumphantly.

Rhodes took the book from him and examined it. It was a Western novel by Justin Ladd, part of a series devoted to the Kansas town of Abilene. The title of this one was *The Cattle Baron.*

"Look at page one forty-nine," Stanley said.

Rhodes put on his glasses, opened the book, located the

correct page, and ran his finger down it to the following sentence:

"   ," one puncher muttered.

"You see?" Stanley said. "The first word in the sentence has been whited out."

"Did you do this, Miz McGee?" Rhodes said, walking over and showing her the book.

She looked at it and then back up at Rhodes. She shook her head. "I never did anything like that, Sheriff. I don't even read shoot-em-ups. I must've picked it up by mistake someway or other. I guess maybe somebody got it mixed in with the Barbara Cartland books."

"Don't let her get away with that, Sheriff," Stanley said. "She must have done it."

"Why?" Rhodes said, closing the book and giving it back to Stanley. "When did she check it out?"

"I, uh . . . " Stanley stopped and thought about it.

"It was four days ago," Miz McGee said. "I remember because it was right at the start of the Easter spell. I always like to have a few good books to read while the Easter spell's blowin'."

"That was before you started to check the books you had on hand to see if they were already marked," Rhodes told Stanley. "You didn't start that until today, remember?"

"I, uh, may have been somewhat overzealous, actually," Stanley said.

"Somewhat my foot," Hack said. "I think we oughta lock him up for false arrest."

"I didn't actually arrest anyone," Stanley said, looking worried. "I just brought her here to the jail. I was hoping you'd arrest her."

"Same thing," Hack said. "How about harassment or somethin', Sheriff? There oughta be some way an innocent woman can protect herself against gettin' hauled down to the jail by a crazy man."

Stanley drew himself up straight. "I am not a crazy man," he said.

"Maybe not," Lawton said, "but you sure was actin' like one."

"I'm sorry," Stanley said. "I really am. I apologize to Miz McGee. It's just that I was so upset by this matter that I let myself get carried away. I promise that it won't happen again."

"It better not," Hack said, looking at Rhodes. "Ain't that right, Sheriff?"

"It wouldn't be a good idea," Rhodes said. "You can't be dragging in everyone who reads a book. I know you're upset, but try doing what I said before you get so enthusiastic about dragging people to the jail."

"I will," Stanley said. "Can I go now?"

"You can go," Rhodes said. "What about you, Miz McGee? You want him to take you back to the library?"

Miz McGee shook her head.

"She sure don't," Hack said. "I'll see that she gets home all right. We might want to go out for a bite to eat later, anyhow."

That was good enough for Stanley, who seemed relieved that he wouldn't have to face Miz McGee alone. He took the book from Rhodes and left hastily.

Before the door closed behind Stanley, Rhodes looked out and saw that the crowd of reporters had thinned noticeably.

"Too late in the afternoon," Lawton said when Rhodes remarked on the reduced numbers. "They got to get back to Waco and Dallas and Houston and all like that to do their stories on the air. Won't be able to make it by six-thirty as it is, not if they go out to Obert and get some shots of the college. They'll have to go some even to get their stuff on the air at ten."

"Red Rogers is still out there, though," Rhodes said. "He doesn't have to worry about things like that."

"If those reporters can stir things up enough," Hack said, "we'll be havin' us a visit from the Texas Rangers."

Rhodes nodded. He didn't want that to happen. He liked to be in control of his own investigations, and if the Rangers came in, he would have to give the case over to them. Later, if he found that he needed help, he could call the Rangers, but he would like for it to be his own choice.

"Why would the Rangers be coming here, and who were all those people?" Miz McGee said. She had not heard about Graham's death, living out of town as she did. Hack told her about Graham and about Rhodes and Brame finding the body.

"My land," she said. "Was he murdered?"

"We don't know yet," Hack said. He wasn't sure whether he should tell Miz McGee that he did know. "Do we, Sheriff?"

"Not for publication," Rhodes said, just as Red Rogers opened the door and came back in.

"I see that all the department business is over," Rogers said. "So tell us, Sheriff, how soon can we expect an arrest in the Graham murder?"

"I didn't say it was murder," Rhodes reminded him.

"You didn't say it wasn't, either," Rogers said. He was young, but he wasn't stupid.

"We'll keep on investigating," Rhodes said. "You'll be the first to hear if we find out anything."

"I know," Rogers said. "Everyone else has left."

Rhodes was glad to hear it. He had enough to worry about without reporters dogging his footsteps. Rogers alone was bad enough.

Knowing that he wasn't going to get any more information, Rogers left, too, just before the phone rang. Hack answered it, and then Rhodes had even more to worry about. It was Oma Coates, and she wanted Rhodes to come out to her house. There was someone there who wanted to talk to him.

"Ask her who it is," Rhodes told Hack.

Hack asked, but Miz Coates wouldn't say. "She just says to come on out there. And to bring your woman deputy."

"Where's Ruth?" Rhodes said.

"There was some trouble between two fellas about a dog poisoning in Milsby. She's over there tryin' to get it straightened out before they beat each other up."

Rhodes looked at the clock over his desk. It was four-thirty. "I'll take Ivy," he said. "If she'll volunteer."

Ivy had not started supper, so she didn't mind driving out to Obert with Rhodes. On the way, he told her about his conclusions in Graham's death and about the stolen cattle. He told her about Marty Wallace and Mitch Rolingson as well, though he did not mention Marty's looks.

"It sounds like you've had a busy day," she said as they swung around the wide curve up Obert's Hill. She looked out the car window. "Look at the bluebonnets. There are some primroses, too."

Buttercups, Rhodes thought automatically. But he didn't say it.

Oma Coates met them at her front door, still wearing her letter sweater. She looked closely at Ivy.

"She ain't the deputy," she said.

"No," Rhodes admitted. "She's my wife. But she's worked with me before. You can talk in front of her."

"It's not me that has somethin' to say. Y'all better come on in, I guess."

They went into the living room, which had a slickly waxed hardwood floor. There was a brownish-gold sofa, and a coffee table sat in front of it on a throw rug. There was a Lane recliner near the sofa, facing an old RCA color television set, not turned on. There was also a rocking chair, and that's where the woman was sitting.

It was late afternoon. There wasn't much light in the room, and Rhodes couldn't see the woman's face very well, but he didn't think he knew her.

"This here's Leona Appleby," Oma Coates said.

Leona Appleby looked at Rhodes and Ivy silently.

Oma Coates stood there for a second and then flipped a wall switch. The overhead light came on, and Rhodes could see Leona Appleby's face better. He didn't like what he saw.

Her left eye was swollen nearly shut, and there was a large purple bruise around it. Her lips were swollen, too, and the bottom one was split open. A dark reddish-brown scab had formed on it.

Ivy went over to the woman and knelt down, putting her arm around her shoulder. "Who did this to you?" she said.

The woman remained silent.

"Says it was her husband," Oma Coates said after a few seconds had gone by. "Says it's not the first time."

Not feeling well, Rhodes thought. That's what the daughter had said. Not feeling well.

"You can talk to us," Ivy said. "We won't let anything else happen to you."

"That's easy for you to say. You ain't got to live with the man," Oma Coates said.

"She doesn't have to either," Ivy said.

"Uh-uh-uh," Oma Coates said, shaking her head. "Where's she gonna go, then? You gonna take her in?"

Ivy looked up. "Yes," she said.

They took her to Ivy's house, which had a FOR SALE BY OWNER sign in the front yard. They had hoped to sell it before now, but the real estate market in Clearview was not exactly on the boom.

"No one will bother you here," Ivy said as she showed Leona Appleby around the house. She pointed out where the towels were and apologized that she had taken the best ones with her when she moved.

She also apologized for the fact that there was no food in the house. "We'll bring you some, though," she said.

"I wish you wouldn't go to the trouble." Leona Appleby's voice was soft and subdued.

"It's no trouble," Rhodes said. The whole thing made him uncomfortable, as similar situations had in the past. He could never quite make himself understand why the women who were abused by their husbands didn't simply leave. Just get up and go. He said as much to Leona Appleby, who looked at the floor and said nothing.

Ivy told Rhodes that he should know better by now. "Women in that situation can't get away," she said. "It's not as easy as you men seem to think."

Leona Appleby certainly agreed. "He watched me all the time, and he told me that if I ran, he'd get me. Sooner or later, he'd get me. And when he did, he'd do a lot worse than this." She reached up and touched the tender side of her face with her hand.

Rhodes shook his head. It wasn't that he hadn't seen it before. He had, too often. But how anyone could beat another human being for absolutely no discernable reason was almost beyond his understanding.

"I'm not going to press charges," Leona Appleby said. "It was just that he hurt me so bad this time, I had to get away for a while. If I go back of my own free will, he won't hurt me for leaving. And I have to go back in a day or two. If I don't, he'll start in on Twyla Faye."

Rhodes clenched his fists. "Has he ever done that before?"

"Once, just once. He didn't mean to."

"Yes he did," Ivy said. "And he'll do it again."

"No," Leona Appleby said. "He promised. He won't do it again."

Ivy looked at Rhodes. They both knew rationalization when they heard it.

"Can't you bring him in just on the basis of what we've seen here?" Ivy said.

"I could, if I could find him, but it wouldn't do any good," Rhodes said. "Not if his wife won't testify against him. He'd be out tomorrow, and he'd be mad as a wet hen. It might just make things worse."

Leona Appleby didn't say anything, but Rhodes could tell by looking at her downcast eyes that she agreed with him.

"What about those cows?" Rhodes said. If he couldn't get her to press charges for abuse, he could put Appleby away for something else.

"What cows?" she said.

"The new ones, the ten new ones," Rhodes said.

"He told me he bought those," Leona said.

Rhodes looked at the wall, then at the floor. He wanted to hit something himself. Or someone. Preferably Cy Appleby. He wondered if that made him as bad as Appleby. Maybe it did, but right then he didn't care.

"I'm going to the store," he said. "Anything you need especially?"

Leona Appleby shook her head, not looking at him. "I wish y'all wouldn't go to all this trouble," she said.

"It's no trouble," Ivy said. She turned to Rhodes. "Don't get bologna and Dr Pepper. Get some ground meat and some chicken. Some bread and milk."

Rhodes left, feeling calmer. He rarely allowed himself to get personally involved in official business, though he had always cared about the people involved, but this time his objectivity was in real danger. There had to be some way to get Appleby, and he was going to find it. He told himself that he was going to find it soon.

* * *

It was Ivy, however, who came up with the idea.

"I was reading in the paper about a rape case in Houston," she said as they were driving back home, having made Leona Appleby as comfortable as they could. "They can take the blood or semen samples and prove it came from a particular person, and they can prove paternity by DNA testing. Could you do that with calves?"

Rhodes didn't know. "You mean do some kind of DNA testing on the stolen calves to see if they came from Appleby's bull or Adkins's bull?" He thought about it. It seemed logical enough. "I don't see why that wouldn't work. I'll try to find out tomorrow. Did I ever mention that you were probably a lot smarter than I am?"

"Nope," Ivy said. "But now that you bring it up, I can ride a motorcycle better than you, too."

"You don't have to remind me," Rhodes said. "Where do you want to eat tonight?"

"Tired of meat loaf?"

"No. I just thought you might like to eat out."

"How about the Dairy Queen? They have those Blizzards on sale for ninety-nine cents."

Rhodes thought about his waistline for about a tenth of a second. Then he thought about how a Heath Bar Blizzard would taste. "Sounds good to me," he said.

10

▼

THE NEXT MORNING, RHODES CHECKED WITH HACK ABOUT Miz McGee.

"He took her out and bought her a cheeseburger," Lawton said. "That's his idea of showing her a big time."

"I wasn't talking about what they ate," Rhodes said, thinking that was his idea of a big time, too, that and a Blizzard. It beat the heck out of oat bran. "I was wondering how she was doing, considering everything that happened yesterday."

"She's all right," Hack said. "I don't think she'll be wantin' to borrow any books from the library for a while, though. She was a little bit scared at first. She couldn't figure out what that Mr. Stanley wanted to bring her down here to the jail for."

"She thought she was comin' to see her sweetie," Lawton said.

Hack ignored him. "Anyhow, I told her all about what had happened with the books, and she could understand why Mr. Stanley was so wrought up. She said she wouldn't want anybody messin' with the books *she* reads."

"Ain't no bad words in that kind of book, anyhow," Lawton said.

"How'd you know about that?" Hack said. "You ever read one?"

Rhodes left them to their wrangling and called Dr. Barton Slick, a local veternarian, and asked him about the possibility of DNA testing on the stolen calves.

"Nope," Slick said. "Never work. Some people aren't that sure about how valid it is even in the case of humans. Too complicated, too."

Rhodes sighed. It had seemed like such a good idea. He hated to tell Ivy.

"But we could do the same thing just by blood typing," Slick said. "No problem."

"We can?" Rhodes said.

"Sure. We'd have to send the blood samples to a lab, but the test would prove pretty conclusively whether the calves came from a particular bull. They've been doing things like that for years."

Rhodes thanked Slick and said that he would call him back. Then he called Adkins.

"I don't have no bull," Adkins said.

"Your cows had calves," Rhodes pointed out.

"Yeah. They all get bred by my neighbor's bull. Burt Sammons's Santa Gertrudis. Can't keep that son in the pasture when there's cows to service. He's over the fence like he was half rabbit."

Rhodes didn't bother to point out that it certainly seemed to be to Adkins's advantage to have a neighbor with such a willing bull.

"Do you think your neighbor would let us take a blood sample from his bull?" Rhodes said. He explained why.

"Don't see why not," Adkins said. "You really think this'll work?"

"It's worth a try," Rhodes said. He didn't want to make any promises.

He hung up and made another call, this time to Jack Parry, the county judge. He wanted to get a search warrant.

Parry agreed that the similarity of the cattle in Appleby's pasture to the ones Adkins had lost was sufficient evidence for a warrant. But he wasn't sure a warrant would allow the taking of blood samples from cattle.

"The statutes say you can't take blood from people," he said. "They don't mention cows, but I imagine the same thing would apply to them."

"You're going to tell me that cows are protected by the Constitution, right?" Rhodes said.

"Well, no, but maybe they are by Texas law. Besides, they're the man's property, or at least they're presumed to be until we prove different."

"I'll show Appleby the warrant and ask for his permission to take the blood samples," Rhodes said. "Maybe he'll think the warrant covers that and let me take the samples without causing any trouble about it." Knowing Appleby, however, Rhodes didn't think that was too likely.

"What if he won't?" Parry said.

"I don't know," Rhodes said. "Maybe I'll pistol-whip him."

Parry laughed. He knew Rhodes would never pistol-whip anyone.

Rhodes, on the other hand, wasn't so sure. In Appleby's case, he was willing to make an exception.

"If he won't," Parry said, "you can get a court order. That way you can even get blood from a person."

"I'll do that, then," Rhodes said. Appleby was safe from pistol-whipping. At least for now.

On the way to Appleby's, Rhodes stopped by the college. He had been wondering about a possible connection between Appleby and Graham's murder. As far as Rhodes was concerned, a man who would beat his wife was capable of anything, and Appleby had not seemed to have a good opinion of Graham.

The cars were still parked by the house, but Wallace and

Rolingson were in the main building. Rhodes found them there on the third floor. The police line was still in place, but that obviously had not bothered them in the least.

It wasn't that things were out of place on the third floor; Rhodes couldn't have sworn that anything had been moved. But it still seemed to him when he saw it that the whole floor had been given a thorough going-over.

Marty Wallace greeted him at the door of the office. She was wearing a short-sleeved blue shirt and a pair of cutoff jeans as faded and tight as those Twyla Faye had been wearing the day before. She looked even better than the first time Rhodes had seen her.

"Good morning, Sheriff," she said, reaching out and touching his arm when he reached the office. Her hand was soft and warm.

Rhodes's voice stuck in his throat at first, but he finally managed to get out a "Good morning." Then he said, "Where's Mr. Rolingson?"

"In here," Rolingson said from inside the office.

"Did you find what you were looking for?" Rhodes said.

Marty Wallace smiled at him, her blue eyes sparkling. "We weren't looking for anything. We were just getting everything in order."

"They were looking for *Tamerlane,* you can bet on that," Hal Brame said from the doorway behind them.

Rhodes decided that he would take the ribbon down. It wasn't doing any good anyway, and he really didn't care who visited the floor now. It was too late to worry about that. Besides, he was pretty sure they hadn't found anything. If they had, they wouldn't still be looking.

Marty's eyes hardened at the sound of Brame's voice. "What are you doing here?" she said to Brame.

"Just looking after my interests," Brame said, walking across the room toward them, carefully avoiding the pieces of scaffolding on the floor. "Simon did say that he would give me the opportunity to buy *Tamerlane,* you know."

"You always were a liar, Brame," Rolingson said, coming out of the office. He too was dressed in shorts, and his legs were as impressive as his arms. He looked as if he could bend his leg and crack a coconut between his calf and thigh.

Brame was not intimidated, despite the fact that he was only about half Rolingson's size. "Prove it," he said.

"You know I can't do that," Rolingson said. "Simon's dead, so we can't prove what he said. That's probably why you killed him."

"Did you hear that, Sheriff?" Brame said. "That's libel, isn't it?"

"Slander," Rolingson said. "But I take it back."

"You can't do that," Brame said, clearly not intimidated at all by Rolingson's size.

Rhodes was beginning to enjoy himself. These people certainly didn't like one another; he might be able to find out quite a lot if he kept them stirred up.

"Why would Mr. Brame want to kill anyone?" he said. "Especially Simon Graham?"

"To get *Tamerlane,*" Marty Wallace said. She was standing disturbingly close to Rhodes. "You know Hal's reputation, of course."

"No," Rhodes said. "I don't think so."

"He's a vulture," Marty said. "He knows where all the really prime books are, and if a serious collector ever gets into a real financial bind, he can count on a visit from Hal, who you can bet will have a big roll of cash in his pocket. It's all off the books with Hal. The collector gets the cash, and he gets it faster than he ever would through legitimate channels, but he doesn't get nearly as much as he would if he did things the right way. And Hal gets the books he wants. The thing of it is, he's never had a book like *Tamerlane.*"

"Bitch," Hal Brame said.

"I notice you didn't call it libel," Rolingson said. "You probably didn't have enough cash for *Tamerlane,* though. I don't even know how you heard about it, but Simon would never have sold it to you, no matter how desperate he was."

Brame smiled a tight smile. "Yes he would. If he were desperate enough."

"No," Marty said. "Not to you. He didn't like you very much, Hal. He never did. He thought you were a jealous little sneak."

"And he was right," Rolingson said. "That's the only reason he told you about the *Tamerlane*. So you'd be even more jealous. And this time there was nothing you could do about it."

"What do you mean by that?" Brame said.

"We know about the Byron letters," Rolingson said.

Brame's temper flared. "The *fake* Byron letters. And you know as well as I do that Simon was aware that they were forgeries. He probably forged them himself. Or maybe he didn't. Maybe you did it for him."

Rolingson came through the office door more quickly than Rhodes would have thought possible. For such a big man, he could really move.

He reached Brame in two steps, grabbed the smaller man's shirt front in his fist, and lifted him a foot or so from the floor.

Brame made gagging sounds and kicked his feet uselessly.

Rolingson drew back his other fist.

Marty Wallace was watching breathlessly, the tip of her pink tongue caught between her front teeth. She didn't seem nearly as attractive now.

"Better put him down," Rhodes said before Rolingson could throw a punch that would no doubt have crushed Brame's skull as if it were a wicker basket.

Rolingson didn't even look at Rhodes. "You gonna make me?" he said.

Rhodes was getting tired of people asking him that. "If I have to," he said.

Rolingson considered it for a while. Then he opened his

fist and let Brame go. Brame hit the floor and stumbled backward for a step before gaining his balance.

"Bully," he said.

Marty Wallace was looking speculatively at Rhodes. "You're cute," she said. "But you don't scare."

"That's enough of that crap," Rolingson said. "Look, Sheriff. We're Simon Graham's closest associates, and I was his business partner. We have a right to look through his things, but that little worm there—" he glowered at Brame "—doesn't belong here for any reason at all. I want him out of here right now."

"Just a minute," Brame said. "I think we're letting personalities get in the way of a very important issue here. It's obvious that you and I don't like one another, Rolingson, but that doesn't mean that we don't *need* one another. Suppose you find that copy of *Tamerlane*. Who's going to buy it from you?"

"Not you, butthole," Rolingson said.

"And why not? What if I happen to have a large sum of cash instantly available to me? I happen to know that your own financial position isn't much better than Simon's was. You needed his success, and he didn't have a lot of it lately. You've suffered financially, I'm sure, simply because he did. And I think a lot of those books he was stuck with were ones you bought for him. That can't have helped your reputation very much."

"Maybe," Rolingson said. "That doesn't mean I have to deal with you, though."

"There are a few other things I could say, too," Brame told him, giving a sidelong glance toward Rhodes.

"Mitch," Marty Wallace said. "Can I have a word with you in the office?"

"Huh?" Rolingson looked at her. "Oh. Sure. Excuse us." He and Marty went into the office.

"What was that all about?" Rhodes said.

"Nothing much," Brame said.

"You told him that there were other things you could say. What does that mean?"

"Just that I know more about those forgeries than he thinks I do."

"If you're concealing knowledge of a crime, you're committing a criminal act yourself," Rhodes said, thinking there was more to it than that.

"Nothing like a crime," Brame said, as smiling and persuasive as if he were selling Rhodes a used car. "Nothing like that at all. I might know something about where the paper for the forgeries was obtained, that's all. I don't think you could trace it to anyone specifically."

"You're sure about that."

"I'm sure."

Marty Wallace and Rolingson came out of the office. Rolingson didn't look happy.

"Look," he said. "We don't have the book. Whoever killed Simon probably took it. But if we find it, we might make a deal with you. I'm not promising anything, though."

"I'm not looking for a promise," Brame said. His eyes were alight with what Rhodes took for either greed or the simple desire to get the better of Rolingson. "All I want is the chance to bid on the book. The first chance is the one I would prefer, of course."

"Okay," Rolingson said. "I guess I can go that far."

Marty stood beside him, smiling while he spoke. It was clear that she had somehow talked him into agreeing to let Brame make an offer on the book.

"Fine," Brame said. He looked around the room. "I guess I'll be going now. Ta-ta." He turned and walked back to the door.

When he was gone, Rhodes said, "I'm not at all sure you two have a legal right to be here, much less a right to talk about selling a book that you don't even have yet. If there's a will, it hasn't turned up yet, but I expect we'll be hearing from Graham's lawyer any time now."

"That book doesn't have anything to do with a will," Rolingson said. "If he bought it, he bought it with money from the business, and we were partners. It might have even been in a lot of books *I* bought for him. The book's mine now."

"It must be worth a lot," Rhodes said.

"It is," Marty Wallace said. "A lot."

"I hope you find it, then," Rhodes said.

"We will," Rolingson said. "Trust me."

Rhodes didn't trust Rolingson at all, but he was more worried about Cy Appleby, and it was time for him to meet Dr. Slick at the pasture. He drove down the hill, wondering if there was any way that Appleby could have known the value of the Poe book. Any man who would steal cows and beat his wife would certainly murder someone for a book that valuable, but Appleby didn't strike Rhodes as the sort of man who would be interested in rare American first editions. So why would he have taken the book?

There were several other questions about Graham's murder that were nagging at the back of Rhodes's mind, but he didn't have time to consider them at the moment. He had to see about blood-typing the calves.

Dr. Slick was waiting beside a blue Ford pickup with two burly assistants when Rhodes arrived at the Appleby house. Appleby's truck was not in the yard, and no one appeared on the porch when Rhodes called out, so he finally had to walk across the muddy yard. His feet did not sink into it as Appleby's had, but it was still unpleasant.

Rhodes stepped up on the porch and knocked on the door facing with his knuckles. "Anybody home?" he called through the screen door.

There was no answer, but in a few seconds Twyla Faye emerged from the dimness inside.

"What do you want?" she said from behind the screen. She did not open the door.

"I want to talk to your father," Rhodes said.

"He's not here. Is that all?"

"No," Rhodes said. "That's not all. I know why your mother wasn't feeling well yesterday, and I know what your father did to her. I want the two of you to get out of this place and talk to a counselor. I have somewhere you can stay."

He and Ivy had talked over the idea during their high-fiber breakfast that morning. Ivy had agreed to talk to Leona Appleby, while Rhodes was to speak to Twyla Faye as soon as he had the chance.

Twyla Faye laughed, but it wasn't a pleasant sound. "You think he wouldn't find us?"

"I'll take care of that part," Rhodes said.

"You don't look big enough."

"I'm not asking you to leave right now," Rhodes said. "Just think about it."

"Maybe. Who are those men out there?"

"They're here to take a few blood samples from your cattle," Rhodes told her. He showed her the search warrant. "Is that all right with you?"

"They're not *my* cows."

"Well, it looks as if you're the one in charge here. Where are your brothers?"

"I don't know. I don't try to keep up with those two."

"So you're in charge. Is it all right if we examine the cattle?"

"I guess so. Just don't hurt 'em."

"We won't," Rhodes said. He turned and waved to Dr. Slick, who got into his truck and drove across the yard and up the fence row toward the cows. Mud was flung off the tires and smacked into the underbody of the pickup.

Looking back at Twyla Faye, Rhodes said, "You're sure your father didn't say where he was going?"

"He just said he had some business to take care of. I didn't ask."

Rhodes got the impression that Appleby wasn't someone who would tell where he was going even if he were asked. He would be surprised if Appleby told anyone very much about his comings and goings, even his own family, though he also suspected that it would not be easy to steal ten head of cattle by yourself. And it might not even be necessary to do it alone if you had two big boys like Clyde and Claude around the house.

He looked up the fence row. Dr. Slick and his helpers were out of the truck, and they already had one of the calves roped. Rhodes was glad they didn't need his help. He wasn't much of a hand with a rope.

"I'll be going now," Rhodes told Twyla Faye. "If your father comes home, tell him that I'm looking for him."

Twyla opened the screen and looked at what the vet and his helpers were doing. "I expect he'll be lookin' for you, too," she said.

"I hope so," Rhodes told her.

11

▼

AT THE TOP OF THE HILL, RHODES STOPPED AT OMA COATES'S
house. He'd been thinking about his conversation with her
concerning the night of Graham's death, and he couldn't
rid himself of the feeling that she had been holding out on
him.

When he saw her, however, he forgot what he had been
going to say.

She came to the door carrying a 12-gauge automatic
shotgun. Her right forefinger was curled around the trigger,
and the barrel was cradled in the crook of her left arm.

"Oh," she said when she saw Rhodes. "It's you."

"It's me, all right," Rhodes said. "You don't seem very
glad to see me."

She looked down at the gun. "This ain't for you. You can
come in if you want to." She shouldered the gun, looking
oddly military as she did so, and opened the door for
Rhodes with her right hand.

Rhodes stepped inside and for the first time that morning
got a good look at her.

She was still wearing the letter sweater, but the entire
right side of her face was red and swollen.

"Appleby?" he said.

"Yep. But you don't have to look so worried, Sheriff. He can't hit *me* like that without gettin' hit right back. No man can do that."

"I'm glad to hear it." Rhodes looked at the shotgun. "What did you hit him with?"

Oma Coates smiled and looked at the shotgun. "You think I hit him with this?" She shook her head. "Uh-uh-uh."

"Well, did you?"

"I would have, but I don't generally carry a shotgun to meet visitors. That Appleby knocked early this mornin', and when I opened the door, he jerked open the screen and hit me in the face. Didn't say a word. Just hit me. Pretty good pop, let me tell you."

"But you hit him back."

"I said so, didn't I? But I guess you could say I didn't hit him, exactly. I kneed him, is more like it."

"Kneed him?"

"Right in the family jewels. I wish you could've seen him backin' up. He was suckin' air, too. Looked like he'd swallowed a grapefruit."

Rhodes smiled. He wished he could have seen it, too. "Did he leave after that?"

"Nope. He came right back at me, soon as he'd got his breath, but by then I'd locked the door and gone for the shotgun. He was rattlin' the door when I got back, but when I showed him the shotgun he backed up faster than he did when I kneed him, even if he did have to walk a little crooked and bent over. He knew I'd use it."

"You should have called my office," Rhodes said.

"What for? I didn't need any help."

"I know you didn't. But you still should have called. We could have arrested Appleby for assault."

"Wouldn't do no good. He'd be right back out on the streets in a day."

Rhodes thought that like a lot of other people, Oma Coates watched too much television. There weren't any streets to speak of in Obert. On the other hand, what she said was true enough in principle.

"People like Appleby don't deserve to get away with anything," Rhodes said. "If I pick him up, will you file charges?"

"Nope. He might file on me for kneein' him. Might say I shot at him. Get him a good lawyer, he might keep me in and out of court for years."

"You didn't, did you?"

"Didn't what?"

"Didn't shoot him."

"Nope. But I would've if he hadn't left right fast. And I will if he comes back. How do you reckon that he knew his wife came here?"

Rhodes thought it was probably Twyla Faye who had told, maybe because she was afraid Appleby was going to start in on her if she didn't, but he wasn't sure. "I don't know," he said. "You call if he comes back. Don't shoot him. I want to talk to him."

"Well, now's your chance," Oma Coates said. "If you can catch up with him."

Outside the door a red pickup careened along the road down the hill, gravel spewing from beneath the tires.

"I'll talk to you later," Rhodes said. He jogged out the door and got into his car to follow Appleby.

Appleby was on the porch of his house, threatening his daughter, who was standing toe-to-toe with him.

"You little bitch. You oughta know better'n to let anybody get into that pasture. I'm gonna—"

Rhodes slammed the door of the county car and cut off Appleby's words.

"You're not going to do anything to anybody, Appleby," he said.

Appleby whirled around. "You son of a bitch. This is all your fault. You come snoopin' around here, and ever'body gets upset. My wife goes off and leaves, my boys are off hidin' somewhere—"

Appleby clamped his mouth shut in a tight line. He was apparently tired of talking. He jumped off the porch and charged across the yard at Rhodes.

Rhodes didn't think that even Oma Coates's shotgun could slow Appleby down this time.

"Appleby!" Rhodes said, stepping forward and trying to stop the charge.

Appleby was not listening. He had concentrated all his rage and frustration on Rhodes.

Rhodes tried to step out of the way, but the mud slowed his feet, and he slipped. Appleby plowed into him, wrapping his arms around him and planting his Angels cap squarely in Rhodes's midsection.

Rhodes went back and down, gasping and sliding through the mud on the seat of his pants. Chickens scattered out of the way, clucking loudly in surprise and protest, pin feathers flying. Appleby clung to Rhodes and continued to butt him in the stomach with his head.

Rhodes struggled to get his breath, wishing that he could knee Appleby right where Oma Coates had.

He couldn't, however. Appleby had his legs pinned.

Rhodes jerked an arm free and swung at Appleby's head. He succeeded only in knocking off the baseball cap, exposing the top of Appleby's head, which was shiny, white, and bald. The hair that curled from under the cap was all on the sides of Appleby's head, and it was all he had. There was nothing at all on top.

Appleby was now trying to butt Rhodes in the chin. Rhodes, still struggling for breath, took a handful of the side hair and jerked as hard as he could. None of it came out, but Appleby gave a satisfying yell and loosened his grip.

Rhodes jerked again and this time succeeded in pulling Appleby off and to the side.

Rhodes tried to stand, but Appleby grabbed his legs and pulled his feet out from under him. Rhodes fell again, this time landing full length on his back. The soft mud cushioned his fall, but Appleby, quick as a cat, straddled him and hit him twice in the face with his big hands. The back of Rhodes's head whacked into the mud.

Rhodes could feel his pistol mashing into his back, but he could not reach it. Even if he could have, he wouldn't have drawn it. The fight was silly and stupid, but Rhodes knew that it had to be finished the way it had begun. That was the only thing Appleby would understand.

He grabbed a wad of Appleby's shirt and heaved him to the side, then rolled over to grapple with him.

Appleby tried to force Rhodes's face into the mud, but Rhodes stiffened his neck and resisted. He got a hand on Appleby's muddy face, turned it, and got his fingers in Appleby's nostrils. It was an unpleasant hold, but an effective one. He pulled up, hard, and thought he felt something give.

Appleby yelled and let go of Rhodes. He tried to slither away through the mud, but Rhodes had his fingers hooked firmly in the nostrils.

He got up slowly, first kneeling in the mud, then rising to his feet, pulling Appleby up along with him, forcing his head back and down.

Appleby had his broad back to Rhodes now, and Rhodes slipped his free arm around Appleby's neck.

"Now then, Appleby," Rhodes said, breathing raggedly, "just calm down, and—"

Appleby planted his feet in the mud and pushed back. Rhodes fell again, Appleby on top of him, but didn't lose his grip. He yanked on Appleby's nose as hard as he could, trying his best to tear it off.

Appleby thrashed and screamed on top of him, but Rhodes kept his hold on Appleby's neck and gave another strong yank. He felt the slickness of blood on his fingers. Or maybe it wasn't blood. Maybe it was just mud.

"Arrrggggghhhh!" Appleby said, and then he went limp.

Rhodes waited awhile before trying to get up. He wasn't going to be fooled again. Appleby didn't move.

"Need any help?"

Rhodes looked up. There was mud in his eyes and plastered to his face, but he could see well enough to recognize Dr. Slick and the assistants standing not far away.

"Now now," Rhodes said. He shoved Appleby off and stood up, then pulled Appleby up as well. All the fight was out of him now, and he stood with his head down. There were dark streaks of blood mixed with the mud on his face.

"How long have you three been standing there?" Rhodes asked Slick.

"We just got here," Slick said. "We'd have come back sooner if you'd just told us there was going to be mud wrestling."

"I hadn't planned on it, to tell the truth," Rhodes said. "Did you get what you came for?"

"Sure did. The calves cooperated a lot better than your friend here."

"He's not my friend," Rhodes said, muscling Appleby toward the car. He stepped on something and looked down. It was Appleby's cap. He decided to leave it there.

Appleby mumbled something that sounded like, "Ah'ahnt mah cap."

Rhodes bent down and picked up the cap. They had rolled on top of it, and the bill was permanently cracked in the middle. There were mud and chicken droppings mashed into the felt, and the red *A* was almost covered with mud. Or something.

Rhodes put the cap on Appleby's head, not trying to straighten it.

"Feel better now?" he said.

Appleby nodded, and Rhodes got him to the car, opened the back door, and helped him get inside.

"How long for that lab report?" he asked Slick.

"Maybe tomorrow if we can get the samples out on a bus this afternoon."

"Good. You all can go on now. Give me a call when you get the results."

"Right." Slick and his partners got into the pickup. Slick leaned out the window. "Anytime you need any help subduing a suspect, just let us know. We're available."

Rhodes managed a grin. "Thanks. I will."

They drove out of the yard, and Rhodes looked toward the porch. Twyla Faye was standing there.

"Have you had time to think about what I talked to you about earlier?" he said.

"I've thought about it some. Mama can come home, now, can't she?"

"As long as I have your father, I guess so. But I still think she needs counseling."

"I'll talk to her about it," Twyla Faye said. "Maybe we'll do it."

"What about your brothers?" Rhodes said. "What's this about them being off hiding somewhere?"

"They go off like that all the time," Twyla Faye said, looking off toward the pasture, avoiding Rhodes's gaze. "They'll be back."

"I want to talk to them, too," Rhodes said. He didn't think the twins would be afraid of their father. There had to be another reason they were avoiding the house.

"I'll tell 'em," Twyla Faye said.

Rhodes didn't know whether to believe her or not.

He got into the car. Appleby was slumped in the back seat behind the mesh. He didn't say anything when Rhodes looked back, and he didn't say anything all the way back to Clearview.

Rhodes knew that he looked a sight. There was mud in his hair, mud on his face, and mud all over his clothes. There were other things, too, like little bits of straw and an occasional chicken's pin feather. The only thing he had to be thankful for was that he hadn't gotten stabbed by a piece of baling wire. There was no telling what kind of bacteria from the yard might have gotten into an open cut.

In spite of the way he looked, Rhodes really didn't think Hack had any call to laugh so hard. Lawton came in, too, and they were both so tickled that Rhodes didn't think they would be able to get Appleby booked.

"Assaultin' an officer," Hack said. "I can see that, all right. What did he assault you with? A compost pile, or a hog pen?"

Lawton, who didn't get such a kick out of Hack's wit as a general rule, seemed to think that was one of the funniest things he'd heard in years.

"Don't get choked," Hack warned him. "The sheriff might have to give you CPR, and Lord knows what-all he's got on his clothes."

Lawton thought that was funny, too, and he laughed even harder.

Appleby didn't think any of it was funny. Mostly he whined about his nose and demanded a doctor.

"First thing you need's a good shower," Lawton said. "Come right on, Mr. Appleby. You're gonna like our little jail."

"You want me to call the doctor for him?" Hack said when Lawton had led Appleby off to his cell. "We don't want to get ourselves sued again."

"You can call the doctor," Rhodes said. "What else has been happening today?"

Hack looked at him critically. "You right sure you want

me to tell you? Right now, I mean. You look to me like you could use you a hot bath."

"I'll bathe later. What about it?"

Hack told him, but the day's activities didn't amount to much, unless you counted another incident at the Covered Wagon.

"Fran Newly again?" Rhodes said.

"Yep," Hack said. "She went out to dump some trash, and sure enough—she's done been mooned again."

Rhodes didn't think Fran had been mooned in the first place, technically speaking, so she couldn't have been mooned again; but he didn't try to explain that to Hack.

"Is she in the habit of going out there every morning?" he said.

"What're you tryin' to say? You tryin' to say Fran went out there *hopin'* to see that fella again? I'm disappointed in you, Sheriff."

"Well, did she?"

Hack laughed. "Prob'ly did, truth to tell. Anyway, she saw 'im. He scooted off just as quick as he did the first time, though, or maybe quicker. You know how a fella can scat in them tennis shoes."

Rhodes didn't know. He hadn't owned a pair of tennis shoes since childhood, and he hadn't been able to run very fast in them even then.

"Have Buddy drive by there late tonight," he told Hack. "See if he can make an arrest before morning."

"Lordy," Hack said. "You know what Buddy's like. Sometimes I think he has the idea dogs and cats oughta wear clothes. You don't think he'll hurt the fella, do you?"

"He knows better than that," Rhodes said. Buddy was a good deputy, even if he was a little prudish. "I'm going home and clean up. Phone me if you need me."

"I'll sure do that," Hack said. Then before Rhodes got out the door, Hack called to him. "Hey, Sheriff, I was wonderin' one thing."

Rhodes turned back. "What?"

"Where do you reckon that nekkid fella spends the day?"

Rhodes opened the door and went out. He could hear Hack laughing as the door swung shut.

12

▼

THE MUD WAS BEGINNING TO DRY, AND LITTLE FLAKES OF IT dropped off Rhodes's pants as he walked toward the car. He ran his hand through his hair and knocked out some more of it. Not enough to help much, though.

Rhodes got into the car, hoping that he wasn't the one who was going to have to clean the interior later. His ribs ached, and he hoped they weren't cracked again. He'd just gotten over the last time.

As he settled himself behind the wheel, he looked over on the passenger side and noticed the Sunday supplement he'd taken from Graham's house at Obert. It was time he read the article for himself, just to see if there was any more information he could get from it.

He could do that at home, however.

After he'd had a bath.

Rhodes decided on a shower rather than a bath. He didn't like the idea of soaking in water that was full of whatever he'd washed off his body, especially considering where his body had been this time. He let the hot water run over him for at least five minutes before switching to cold, and he still didn't feel entirely clean. For some reason he kept thinking about the chickens, and he wasn't even sorry he wasn't allowed to eat eggs anymore.

After he'd dried off and changed clothes, he put the clothing he'd removed into the washing machine, poured in some liquid detergent, and started the cycle.

After that he cleaned and oiled his pistol. It was a dirty job, and he wished he'd done it before taking the shower. It took him almost an hour.

Then he went into the kitchen for something to eat.

There was still some meat loaf left, so he made a sandwich. It was either that or cereal, and he'd had about as much fiber as he wanted for the day, except for what he got in the sandwich. Ivy would not buy white bread, so Rhodes had no choice but to go for the loaf made of oat bran. It wasn't bad, but there were times when Rhodes craved the taste of the puffy white airiness that he was used to, even if it had been scientifically proved that rats fed an exclusive diet of white bread all died of malnutrition.

While he ate, he flipped the pages of the Sunday supplement until he came to the article about Graham. There was a color photo of Graham's shop in Houston and another of the college campus, looking much more impressive than it did in reality. Graham was standing in front of the main building in his professional Texan outfit, and wildflowers were blooming in profusion in the grass around him. That made the picture at least a year old.

Rhodes got his glasses out of his pocket. They hadn't been broken in the fight, but he had to straighten the right earpiece. When he had done that, he put the glasses on and started reading the article.

He didn't find out anything that he didn't already know, except for a name of a San Antonio bookman, Willie Scott, who was apparently the author's main source of information about the book business in general and Simon Graham in particular. Rhodes thought it might be a good idea to talk to Scott. After all, the information he'd gotten from Wallace, Brame, and Rolingson came from highly prejudiced sources.

Rhodes went out into the backyard and checked Speedo's water. It was another warm day, and Speedo was lying in the shade of a tall pecan tree on a patch of cool earth that he had scratched free of grass. Speedo didn't like warm weather; he preferred the depths of winter to even the touch of summer. His tongue lolled out of his mouth, and he didn't even bother to get up to greet Rhodes, though his tail did make a couple of light thumps on the bare ground.

After filling the water bowl, Rhodes brushed as much of the dried mud as he could off the car seat and drove to the courthouse. He used his office there only occasionally, generally at times he did not want to be disturbed, and this was one of those times.

He walked through the cool halls and up the stairs. He unlocked the office door and went inside. It was dim and shadowy in the room, but Rhodes didn't turn on the fluorescent lights. He liked the dimness, the weak light coming in through frosted glass. He sat at his desk and dialed information to get Scott's number.

Scott was a little suspicious at first, and Rhodes offered to let him call back.

"I can give you the number, but you'd probably rather get it yourself, just to be sure," Rhodes said. "Ask for the Blacklin County Sheriff's Office. Not the jail." He gave Scott the area code.

"You must be on the level or you wouldn't give me a chance to call back," Scott said. "I'll go ahead and talk to you if you think it will help in some way. I'm not sure I can tell you anything germane to Simon's death, however."

"It's some other people that I want to know about," Rhodes said. "People associated with Graham."

"Oh," Scott said. "You probably mean Mitch Rolingson. And Marty Wallace."

"Two out of three," Rhodes said.

"I can't think of any other associates," Scott said.

"How about a man named Hal Brame?"

"I wouldn't exactly call him an associate. More like a rival."

"That's the kind of thing I want to know," Rhodes said. "But there's something else I want to ask you about first." He told Scott about *Tamerlane.*

"I'd heard that rumor," Scott said. "I didn't believe it, of course, but the really interesting thing about the book business is that you never know what might turn up in some old attic or barn. It's just barely possible that Simon could have found a copy. God knows where it came from, but it's still a possibility. It would be quite a coup if he had."

That was pretty much what Brame had said earlier. Too bad that the book would not do Graham any good now even if he had found a copy.

"How much would it be worth?" Rhodes said. "About."

"It's really hard to give a definite answer to that question, Sheriff," Scott said. "The value of a rare book depends on a number of factors. Condition, for example, would be very important, though with a book as difficult to obtain as the *Tamerlane,* that might not matter as much as it would with a more recent publication."

"I don't have to have an exact figure," Rhodes said. No one seemed to want to commit to a dollar amount. He wondered if that were a characteristic of book dealers everywhere. "Just some kind of a ballpark estimate will do."

"Very well, then," Scott said. "Let's say somewhere in the neighborhood of a quarter of a million dollars."

Rhodes whistled. He had gathered that the book was valuable, but he hadn't expected that it would be worth *that* much.

"Are you sure?" he said.

"I told you," Scott said, "that it would depend on a lot

of different things. It could be worth as little as a hundred and fifty thousand. It could go even higher than a quarter of a million if you found the right buyer and if everything else was right."

Rhodes was stunned at the amount of money involved, but he had something else to ask. "There's something else I'd like your opinion on," he said.

He started to tell Scott about the Byron letters, but Scott interrupted him. "I know all about those letters, Sheriff. Everyone in the business does."

"Tell me, then," Rhodes said. "How is something like that done?"

Scott explained that paper of the proper age could be obtained from old, but not necessarily rare, books of the same era that the letters were supposed to come from.

"The endpapers could be cut out, for example. And the handwriting could be forged even by a skillful amateur. It's the ink that would give trouble, and it did in this case. It's not easy to find ink that was made in the early part of the nineteenth century."

"But it almost worked," Rhodes said.

"Almost," Scott said. "But not quite."

"Then what I want to know is, could a man forge a whole book like this *Tamerlane?*"

There was silence on the line while Scott thought about it.

"That's an interesting question," he said after a moment. "Especially considering what we're discussing here. The age of the paper used in those letters would be just about right for *Tamerlane.* Not exactly, but close. And of course *Tamerlane* isn't a book, precisely. Not in the modern sense. It's more like something we might call a pamphlet."

There was another silence while Rhodes and Scott both considered the implications of all that.

"What are you getting at, Sheriff?" Scott said then.

Rhodes wasn't sure himself. He changed the subject to Mitch Rolingson.

"Rolingson is a good book hound. He finds things, in large quantities sometimes. But they aren't always good things, and sometimes he buys an enormous collection to get one or two valuable items. Then he and Simon would be stuck with a huge and not very desirable inventory."

"That's the case now, isn't it?" Rhodes said.

"So I've heard."

"Unless Graham found something like this *Tamerlane* stashed away in that inventory," Rhodes said.

"Yes," Scott said. "Something like that would make a rather large difference."

"Have you heard whether either Rolingson or Graham was involved in forging those letters?" Rhodes said, getting back on track.

"There are always plenty of tales floating around in this business," Scott said. "I don't intend to repeat them, however. No one seems to know conclusively, anyway, and there are strong arguments on both sides. Personalities enter into it, as they usually do. Rolingson has suffered a lot from his association with Graham. It won't be easy for him to make a go of it as a book dealer from now on, not unless he can convince people of his innocence."

"What about Hal Brame?"

"What do you mean?"

"He seems to have an interest in this *Tamerlane,* but Rolingson doesn't like him very much. Marty Wallace may not like him either, but she made Rolingson promise to let him look at the book, maybe buy it."

"Brame is an interesting character," Scott said. "Not entirely reputable, in a sense, though plenty of people deal with him. He's always on the edge, but no one has ever actually caught him crossing the line. He always seems to make money and to have plenty of it available."

Scott paused for a moment as if thinking about how to

put what he was going to say next. Then he went on. "As I mentioned, there are a lot of tales floating around in the book trade, and one of them has it that Brame bought some books from Graham, books that he later discovered had missing endpapers. So when he heard about the letters, he spread the word immediately that they might be forged. No one could prove that it was Graham who removed the endpapers, of course, and he *did* make restitution."

"But it didn't help him any financially. He didn't have any reason to like Brame."

"No, and neither would Rolingson. There's also a rumor that Brame tried to imply that Rolingson was implicated as well, but no one bought it."

"And then there's Marty Wallace."

"You sound a little wistful, Sheriff."

"I'm a married man," Rhodes said.

"Yes. That's enough to make anyone wistful if he comes in contact with Marty. She looks wonderful, doesn't she."

Rhodes admitted it.

"But that's as far as it goes. She associated with Simon primarily because of his social contacts and his money. Now, thanks to Brame, he's lost a lot of both. She wouldn't have stayed with him much longer, even if he hadn't died."

"She's here, now, though," Rhodes said.

"Then she believes the *Tamerlane* is real. You can count on it. One thing that the lovely Marty likes is money."

"Would any one of those three have a reason to kill Graham?"

"Good Lord, Sheriff. I thought he committed suicide."

"I didn't say he didn't. I was just asking a hypothetical question."

Scott paused for thought again. Finally, he said, "Very well. I'll give you a hypothetical answer. All of them. If they thought they could get away with it and get their hands on *Tamerlane.*" There was a stretch of silence. "I don't suppose you collect books, Sheriff."

"No," Rhodes said. He thought about Ballinger. "I know someone who does, though."

"It's like a disease in a way," Scott said. "It's not just the money, you know, though that's a part of it. It's also the fact of the book itself, possessing it, knowing that you have a copy of something that other people would literally kill for if it's rare enough. There's great pleasure in owning something like that. Of course, dealers don't generally experience that kind of pleasure. They like to think they keep themselves above it while they cater to the pleasure of others."

Rhodes had collected baseball cards when he was a kid. He could almost understand what Scott was talking about. There were some he traded; there were others he would never have parted with for any amount of money.

"Sometimes I wonder if *I* wouldn't kill for a book like that," Scott said. "Not to have it, of course. Or at least not to have it for long. But to be able to say I had it and sold it, well, that would be something. Once in a lifetime."

"Brame might feel that way, then," Rhodes said.

"Perhaps. Maybe even Rolingson. Not Marty, however. She would care only about the money."

Rhodes talked to Scott for a bit longer, but he didn't learn anything else that seemed helpful. After hanging up, he went down the hall to the Dr Pepper machine, got a bottle, stuck it into the opener and yanked off the top. He wondered why it was so much more satisfying to do that than it was to pop the top on a can or twist the cap off a two-liter plastic bottle.

He went back to the office then, put his feet on the scarred top of his desk, and leaned back in the chair. As he sipped the drink, he tried to go through everything again, point by point, to see if he could put his finger on all the little things that were bothering him about the entire affair.

It was quiet in the courthouse in the afternoon. Rhodes heard the far-off hum of the air-conditioning unit. He listened to someone's high heels clicking down the hall. And as he listened, one of the things that had been bothering him came into focus.

He should have thought of it sooner, but too much had happened in too short a time, even though it had been obvious from the beginning. How did Hal Brame hear what he said he'd heard? When he came to the jail, he said that it wasn't just the lights that had frightened him at the college that night. There were also the sounds, the ghostly groans.

There was no way Brame could have heard any groans, not if he had been outside the building. The windows had been closed, and the wind had been blowing a gale. Graham had died on the third floor, very high up and a long way from where Brame said his car was parked.

No one had hearing that good. Of course, Brame could have added the part about the groans to get Rhodes's attention and to make sure he investigated the lights.

Rhodes went back over the whole evening in his mind. One other incident stuck out. He had been about to leave the third floor when Brame grabbed his arm and called his attention to the rat. Had Brame really been frightened, or was he just trying to call Rhodes's attention to the hanged man, who Brame had known was hanging there all along?

And if the office had been locked that night, how had Marty Wallace gotten in the next day? If the keys had been taken from Graham, had she taken them? Or had someone else? And where were the keys, anyway? Rhodes still hadn't seen them.

None of these questions fit with Rhodes's pet theory, which was simply that Cy Appleby was the killer. Appleby fit the profile. He was violent, he was a thief, he was an abuser. Graham could have seen something from the third floor that Appleby wanted to keep hidden; Appleby had implied as much.

Suppose Graham had been on the third floor and seen

Appleby unloading a trailer full of cattle in the middle of the night. Even a book dealer might have become suspicious of something like that. And suppose he had said something about it to Appleby.

Appleby was the kind of man who would murder under those circumstances, Rhodes thought.

He really wanted it to be Appleby.

But what about Clyde and Claude? Where were they? Why had they run away? Had *they* killed Graham?

It wasn't impossible. They worked for him on the third floor. Suppose they had seen the copy of *Tamerlane* and asked Graham about it. He might have played the big man, told them its real value. That would have been quite a temptation to two boys like Claude and Clyde. They might not have realized until it was too late that they were unlikely to have the contacts to sell it.

Rhodes then thought of another scenario, one he liked even better. This one had Claude and Clyde telling their father about the book. It had them going into hiding because the sheriff had come looking for their father, whom they knew to be guilty of Graham's murder.

The more he thought about that idea, the better he liked it; it explained everything, and more. It explained why Brame, Wallace, and Rolingson hadn't been able to find the book.

That was it, all right. Rhodes was sure of it.

Now all he had to do was find the twins.

He might have looked for them then, but he was distracted.

When he drove by the jail to check in with Hack, he found out that Buddy had captured the flasher.

And then he found out that someone had killed Oma Coates.

13

▼

"WHERE YOU BEEN?" HACK SAID WHEN RHODES ENTERED THE jail. He was unusually agitated. "I been callin' all over."

"Did you try the courthouse?"

"I was about to. We got us a mess here."

"What's the trouble?"

"Buddy caught up with the fella who's been sleepin' behind the dumpster at the Covered Wagon."

"Good. Did he bring him in?"

Hack nodded. "He sure did. That's not the trouble."

"Well, what is?" Lawton wasn't around, and Rhodes thought he might actually get a direct answer.

"He had to chase him on foot."

Rhodes said that he didn't really see anything wrong with that.

"Nothin' wrong with it?" Hack said. "You know where the Covered Wagon is?"

Rhodes knew.

"Well, Buddy pulled up behind it, in the alley close to the dumpster. He checked ever'thing out, but there wasn't nobody there. He was just about to leave when he decided to check out the old Sinclair fillin' station up the block. You know which one I mean?"

Rhodes nodded. The old white-painted brick station was a familiar sight in Clearview. Although it had not been in operation for fifteen or twenty years, there was still a sign with a faded green dinosaur on it hanging out front. There was no longer any glass in any of the windows, and the two overhead doors to the garage section had long since disappeared, along with the doors to the rest rooms.

"And that's where the man stays during the day," Rhodes guessed. "In the Sinclair station."

"That's right. He must've seen Buddy coming, though, and he took off like a scalded dog, right up the street. And all he had on was those tennis shoes. Well, them and the socks, not that the socks made much difference."

Rhodes thought about that. The Covered Wagon was several blocks from the main section of the town, but Hack would not be so upset if Buddy had caught up to the man within a short distance.

"Did he get downtown?" Rhodes said.

"He sure did. I guess those tennis shoes did make him able to run fast, like I said. By the time Buddy caught up with him, he'd passed the furniture store and the drugstore. The church, too."

"I imagine a lot of people saw him," Rhodes said.

"Some lady in the drugstore fainted," Hack said. "I don't think she'd ever seen anything like that."

"Maybe it was the tennis shoes," Rhodes said.

"This ain't funny anymore, Sheriff," Hack said. "Buddy had to hold him pressed against that plate-glass window in the front of the drugstore while he cuffed him. Then he marched him back to the patrol car."

"Right past the whole town," Rhodes said.

"You bet. I got a call from Billy Lee down at the drugstore. He was a little depressed about that woman faintin' on the premises, but considerin' what was pressed up against that window, he wasn't too surprised that it happened."

"That's not good," Rhodes said.

"I know somethin' worse," Hack said.

"What could that be?"

"Red Rogers was in the drugstore."

Rhodes could only guess what Clearview's intrepid reporter would have to say about the incident, especially considering that it came right on the heels of Graham's murder. He decided not to tune in to the local station for a day or two. The trouble was that most of the county commissioners could be counted on to be among the listeners even if Rhodes wasn't.

"Did we get him booked?" he said.

"Lawton's settlin' him in right now. We got him a jailhouse outfit to wear, so at least he's decent."

"He give any reason for being dressed the way he was?"

"Says he's one of Blacklin County's homeless. Says he can't afford anything to wear, and it's all society's fault. Says he has the shoes because he found 'em in somebody's trash pile. Says he was looking for somethin' to wear in the dumpster behind the Covered Wagon."

"Did you tell him he wouldn't be very likely to find it there?"

"Sure did, but he said he didn't care. Said the food they throw out there is the best in town. He hopes it'll be better here in the jail, though."

"It will," Rhodes said. Miz Stutts, who provided the meals for the jail, was the best cook in town. The flasher, or whatever the right term for him was, wouldn't have any complaints on that score.

Rhodes talked to Hack for a bit longer and finally convinced him that the excitement would soon die down. He was about to leave the jail when the phone rang.

It was Twyla Faye. She sounded panicky, and it took Hack a minute to get her to slow down and tell him what she wanted.

What she wanted was to tell someone that Oma Coates was dead.

Twyla Faye had spent the day thinking over what Rhodes had said, and she had decided that she wanted to talk to her mother. If her mother would go to the counselor, then Twyla Faye would go with her. It wouldn't hurt to try it, not while Appleby was in jail, at least. There was nothing he could do to them while he was there.

The Applebys didn't have a phone, so Twyla had gone to Oma Coates's house to call the sheriff. She heard scuffling inside the house when she got there, and she heard a weak call for help.

She opened the door, which was unlocked, and called out. There was a crash in the kitchen, and the back door slammed shut. She went into the kitchen. That was where she found Oma Coates, lying on the floor, dead.

Miz Coates had been strangled.

Twyla Faye had told Rhodes all of this in between sobs after he arrived at the house. Her flippant toughness had not been more than skin deep. Miz Coates's murder had stripped it away, partly, Rhodes thought, because Twyla Faye for the first time realized what her own father's violent behavior might one day lead to. He had arranged with Ruth Grady to drop her off at Ivy's house.

Rhodes inspected the scene. The shotgun that Miz Coates had been carrying when she came to the door earlier in the day was now leaning in a corner by the kitchen stove. It hadn't helped her at all when the time came. She was still wearing the same sweater.

After looking through the house and finding nothing else that seemed relevant to the murder, Rhodes searched the surrounding area, but no one had anything helpful to report. No one in any of the closest houses, which were all more than a block away, had seen or heard anything out of the ordinary. They were all shocked and outraged to hear of the murder of Oma Coates.

Rhodes visited Mitch Rolingson and Marty Wallace last. They were watching a game show on television.

"Didn't hear a thing," Rolingson said. "We were just taking a break from inventorying Simon's collection."

By that Rhodes understood him to mean that they were still searching for *Tamerlane* but that they hadn't found it.

"You didn't see anyone drive up to the Coates house? You didn't hear a car?"

"Not a thing," Marty Wallace said. "It might have happened while we were over there in the other building, up in the office. We just got back here a few minutes ago. You don't think that woman's death had anything to do with what happened to Simon, do you?"

Rhodes didn't know, but it certainly seemed likely. He wasn't much of a believer in coincidences.

"Good Lord," Marty said. "That's horrible. I hope you catch whoever did it."

"And soon," Rolingson said. "I'm beginning to believe that this isn't a very healthy place to be."

Rhodes left them there. Ruth Grady had come and taken Twyla Faye to Ivy's house to be with her mother, and Oma Coates's body had been taken to Ballinger's Funeral Home.

Rhodes went back to the kitchen and the scene of the struggle. It was clear that there had been someone else there with Miz Coates. There had been a cup of coffee on the table. The killer had thrown Oma Coates down, and she had hit the table. The coffee cup had overturned and coffee had run across the Formica tabletop and onto the floor. The table had been knocked up against the stove at the side of the room.

Who the visitor was, or why he or she had been there, Rhodes didn't know.

One thing he did know, however, was that he was going to have to start looking for another killer.

Or maybe Oma Coates's killer was the same one who had murdered Graham.

If so, that eliminated Appleby. Rhodes was sorry about that. He had really hoped to put Appleby away in the TDC for a long time.

The elimination of Appleby left Rhodes wondering even more about Brame. Oma Coates had seen Brame's car at the college the night Graham died. Had she seen something else? Rhodes recalled again that she had appeared to be holding something back when he had first talked to her. He wished now that he had taken the opportunity to press her a little harder, but he had thought there would be time for that later.

He should have known better, but it was too late to scold himself about that now. She might not have told him, and even if she had, what she said might not have meant anything.

On the other hand, it might have saved her life.

It was easy to say that what happened to her was her own fault, but Rhodes couldn't shake the notion that he was at least partly to blame.

He would do what he could to set things right, but he knew that he could never really do quite enough. Oma Coates would never shake her head at anyone again.

Before he left the house and drove to the Lakeway Inn, he used the telephone to call Ivy at work. He told her what had happened and asked her to go by and check on Twyla Faye and her mother.

"I suppose this means you won't be home until late," Ivy said.

"Probably not. I hope you don't mind going by and looking in on those two."

"I don't mind. In fact, I want to. But I can't seem to get used to the idea of not having you around every evening. I was worried about that before we married, you know."

"I know," Rhodes said. "I'll get there as soon as I can."

"See that you do," Ivy said. But Rhodes could tell that she was smiling when she said it. Or he hoped she was. He didn't feel quite so bad when he got into his car and drove away.

"Checked out?" Rhodes said. "When?"

The motel clerk, who looked about seventeen, looked at the monitor of his computer. As Hack had often told Rhodes, everybody had one.

"Noon," the clerk said. "Is there something wrong, Sheriff?"

He looked worried, as if the motel's owner would hold him entirely responsible if anything besmirched the good name of the Lakeway Inn.

"I don't know yet," Rhodes said, but he did. There was something wrong, all right, and it was getting more wrong all the time.

Although he'd promised himself he wouldn't tune in the local radio station, Rhodes forgot himself, getting sucked in by a female disc jockey who promised to play two songs by Emmylou Harris back to back. Rhodes was a sucker for Emmylou.

He should have changed the station after the songs, but he didn't, because then the disc jockey played an old Roy Orbison record, and Rhodes couldn't resist Roy Orbison, either, especially when he was singing "Crying."

After that, it was too late to switch. Red Rogers had already come on.

Unfortunately, he had found out about the murder of Oma Coates, which made him suspicious that Simon Graham, "a near neighbor of the late Mrs. Coates," had also been murdered, "though our elected law officials refuse to speculate on that point."

Then he *really* got going. The gist of Rogers' remarks was that not only was there a murder epidemic in Blacklin

County, but that naked perverts were roaming freely through the public streets, exposing their vulgar selves to the pure matrons of Clearview.

"The shocking spectacle inspired fear and disgust in many Clearview residents, causing one woman to collapse to the floor of a local business establishment. After being rushed to the hospital emergency room, she recovered consciousness and told this reporter, and I quote, 'I'm seventy-two years old, and I never saw anything like it.' "

Well, Rhodes thought, Hack had been right about that.

There was more to the broadcast, with Rogers declaiming in his best imitation–Paul Harvey voice, but Rhodes didn't listen. He twisted the knob until he got a country station out of Dallas that was playing cuts off a new Clint Black album. Rhodes thought Black was one of the best things to happen to country music since Randy Travis and Dwight Yoakum had come along, and the songs helped to take his mind off Red Rogers.

They didn't take his mind off other things, though. He got on the police band radio and had Hack start calling Brame's home and shop in Houston.

Then he went looking for Claude and Clyde.

He wished that he had looked for the twins sooner. He was afraid that they might be the ones he should have been looking for all along. They had worked for Graham and spent a lot of time very near Oma Coates's house. She might have seen something, if they were the ones implicated in Graham's murder, and it might have been what she had seen that she was holding back from Rhodes.

They also might have killed her for another reason. Their father had already attacked her, and now he was in jail. Revenge was something that had been very much on Appleby's mind.

Like father, like sons.

Rhodes thought of the marks on Miz Coates's neck, and he thought about the twins' big hands.

He drove back to Obert. It was getting late, and the shadows stretched across the top of the hill. It would stay light at the top longer than it would in the surrounding countryside.

Rhodes had always liked the hill. For one thing it reminded him of the hills he had seen in the B-Westerns of his childhood, and it had everything required for the set of a Republic serial except a cave. As far as Rhodes could recall, every serial he had ever seen had a cave in it.

If there had been a cave on Obert's Hill, that would have been the first place Rhodes would have looked. In a serial, that would be the place where the villain was lurking about in his robe and mask, plotting against the hero. Rhodes wished the world were still as simple as that, with the bad guys wearing such outrageous getups that you couldn't miss them.

Even though there wasn't a cave, however, there was an unusual pile of rocks that might be a good place for the Appleby twins to hide out. Rhodes had no idea how the rocks had come to be there. They were a part of the college grounds, in fact a part of the same field through which Claude and Clyde had fled after taking off down the fire escape, and Graham had no doubt had some plan to work the rocks into his renovations. They would have made an interesting tourist attraction.

Rhodes parked in front of the main building and walked across the field through which Claude and Clyde had made their escape. The ground was soft under his feet, though not as bad as the yard at the Appleby place. The bluebonnets brushed against his pants as he walked along, and he watched for fire ant mounds. He didn't have to worry much about chiggers. The fire ants had eaten them all.

About halfway across the field, Rhodes angled back to his left. He could see the rock pile sticking high out of the ground, green with weeds around the base. There were a few flowers growing there, too, but they were yellow and Rhodes couldn't identify them, though Ivy probably could have. He'd have to ask her.

The rocks were quite large. To Rhodes they looked a little bit like a herd of dinosaurs that had somehow been petrified and left right there in the middle of the field.

He remembered having visited the rocks long ago, and as he recalled there were several of them that were leaning together in such a way that they formed a sort of shelter. While you couldn't call it a cave, it was a place that had looked as if it would stay dry in the rain and keep the wind off if the weather turned cool. On a day like this one, it would provide a comfortable shade.

The only thing Rhodes didn't like about it was the possibility that there were snakes lurking about. He had never seen a rattler in Blacklin County, but if there happened to be one in the vicinity, the rocks would be the best place for it to hide out. If other people felt about snakes the way Rhodes did, they would keep their distance from the rocks, making it an even more attractive place to the Appleby twins.

It was a good theory, but as it turned out the twins weren't there after all. There were signs that someone had been there fairly recently—a couple of aluminum Diet Pepsi cans, some cigarette filters, three pieces of crumpled wax paper that had bread crumbs in them. Someone who had no fear of snakes had probably had a picnic there, not so surprising when you considered the privacy and comfort of the place. It didn't really look so snaky when you got close to it.

Rhodes picked up the cans, paper, and filters to carry away in his car. He didn't like littering.

He was not too disappointed in not finding Claude and Clyde. He hadn't really thought he would find them in the first place he looked. That would have required more luck than he usually had when he was looking for people. There were at least three other places he could search.

There was no one in the first of those two, the college gymnasium. The gymnasium had suffered somewhat less for the passage of time than the other college buildings because it had been used by some of the local kids for pickup basketball games for years before the property was sold to Graham. They had kept it swept out and even made some minor repairs to the floor and walls.

Now it had broken windows, and there were birds' nests in the rafters. And there was no one hiding in it.

The next place was the dormitory, which at present wouldn't really do for anyone to sleep in. The floor was sagging, there were few windows left at all, and Rhodes was sure he could hear rats in the walls. He wouldn't have stayed there himself, and he was pretty sure no one else would either, not as long as there was somewhere else to go.

And there was at least one other place.

There was the Haunted House.

14

▼

THE HAUNTED HOUSE WAS NOT FAR FROM THE COLLEGE, BUT then nothing in Obert was far from anything else. The road that led from Clearview to Obert swung through the town and then made a sharp turn back to the left, cutting off the college, which was reached by driving on one of the town's few streets.

To get to the Haunted House, Rhodes had to drive back to the decaying business district of Obert—only the post office and a small grocery store left—and get back on the highway and head toward the next town, a little place named Gorton, approximately three times Obert's size, which did not qualify it as a metropolis.

About halfway down the hill, Rhodes turned off on a gravel road to the left and drove a quarter of a mile. The Haunted House loomed up on his right.

It was of the same era as the college's main building and made of the same stone, two stories tall and deserted for the past sixty years. There were many tales about the house, and as far as Rhodes knew, some of them might even be true, though he had serious doubts about most of them.

The locals had two favorites. The first had to do with the

house's original occupants, a Mr. and Mrs. Findley. According to the story, Mr. Findley had been a man not entirely unlike Cy Appleby, except that he was fairly well-to-do. Unfortunately, however, he had a penchant for beating his wife, but in his case, since he was a prominent citizen, everyone in town had known what was going on. Things being the way they were in those days, however, no one seemed to want to do anything about it. They figured that Mr. Findley pretty much had a right to do whatever he wanted to do to the woman he was married to.

Mrs. Findley, however, for some reason or another, didn't share the prevailing opinion. One night after a particularly brutal session with her husband, she waited until he was asleep, went out to the woodshed, and got the ax. She even sharpened it. She supposedly told the neighbors later when she wakened them to tell them what she'd done that if she did the job at all, she wanted to do it right.

She'd done pretty well, and the neighbors found the late Mr. Findley hacked into six pieces on the blood-soaked cellar floor—legs, arms, torso, and head.

He was in the cellar, Mrs. Findley explained, because he woke up when she was coming at him with the ax and he had run from her. She didn't know why he hadn't awakened sooner, say when she was sharpening the ax on the grindstone. Anyway, she chased him all through the house, and he might have eventually gotten away if he hadn't stubbed his toe on a rough stone in the cellar floor. He fell down, and that was when his wife finally caught up with him. He never had a chance to get up.

County records showed that Mrs. Findley had never been brought to trial. Folks seemed to think she had as much a right to do unto Mr. Findley as he had had to do unto her, and Rhodes thought there was a kind of rough justice in that.

Several families had lived in the house after Mr. Findley's violent demise, but none had stayed long. There were reports of strange noises in the cellar—ear-splitting screams, the sound of an ax blade ringing on stone. Some people claimed to have been standing outside when those noises occurred, and they swore that they looked through the basement window and saw sparks being struck from the cellar floor. They swore that when they looked inside, they could see the bloodstains bright as new, though other people, just as reliable, had looked later and seen nothing.

The other well-known story was about a man named Laughlin, the last occupant of the house. He kept complaining about the noises he heard at night, saying that he hadn't slept well for weeks. His friends encouraged him to move out, but he'd made a joke about it, saying that no ghosts were going to get his goat.

No one knew what had happened to Laughlin during his last night in the house. He was never able to tell them. When they found him the next morning, he was foaming at the mouth and talking nothing but gibberish, completely insane. The story was that his hair, which had been coal black, had turned entirely white. He never spoke another coherent word.

Rhodes thought that probably half the little communities in Texas had a house like Obert's Haunted House. And probably half of those had the same stories told about them, the same ones or extremely similar ones.

That didn't make the house's legend any less potent. Rhodes or one of the deputies had to go there about once a year, usually around Halloween, to investigate reports of screams or strange lights. There were never any ghosts, never any sign of one, and no tangible trace that anyone had been there. There had certainly never been a hanged man, like the one Rhodes had found in the ghostly college building.

But the legend nevertheless persisted. No one wanted to have much to do with the Haunted House, but Rhodes thought it was possible that Claude and Clyde hadn't heard the stories. They didn't associate much with the people of Obert, and to them the house might have appeared to be nothing more than another deserted building.

Rhodes got out of the car and slammed the door. It was a loud sound in the late afternoon silence. The house was surrounded by old cedar trees that shrouded it in shadow, and the sun was very low. It would be dark in less than half an hour. Rhodes opened the door again and got out his flashlight. He was pretty sure he would need it.

Rhodes looked at the cold stone front, the empty windows and door. He felt a shivery chill run up his back and thought he might be wiser to wait until the next day to go into the house. And that he should get someone to go with him.

Then he laughed at himself. He was a grown man, and he didn't believe a word of those stories about the house. Well, not most of them. Besides, he was warned. And the worst thing he would find in there was the twins.

Rhodes crossed the yard. There were few weeds and very little grass. The shade from the cedars stopped most of the growth.

He reached the four stone steps leading up to the porch. He took them one at a time, listening to the sound his shoes made as they scuffed on the rock. When he got to the top step, he stood silently, listening. There were no sounds from inside the house, no sign of anything suspicious, but that didn't matter, not according to the letter and intent of law, even though there was a NO TRESPASSING sign nailed to the door facing.

Rhodes did not need a probable cause to enter the building. The Haunted House was abandoned property, and as far as the law was concerned that gave Rhodes a right to search it without a warrant, just as he'd searched the gym and the dormitory. The owner didn't have to give up his property rights for the property to be classified as abandoned. The NO TRESPASSING sign didn't apply to law officers.

Rhodes went through the doorway, shining his light on the floor. There was thick dirt in the entranceway, but it had been disturbed. Someone had been walking there, and not too long ago. Rhodes felt sure he was in the right place this time.

He shined the light around. There was a tiny skeleton on the floor, some kind of bird, he thought. It was partially covered with dirt and looked as if it had been there for a long time. There were a few twigs and thin pieces of string nearby, the remains of the bird's nest. Spider webs were thick on the walls.

To Rhodes's right there was a stairway going up. It did not look safe; the railing appeared rotten and was leaning outward at a dangerous angle. The fifth step from the bottom was broken through.

Rhodes walked along the hall beside the stairway. At the back of the stair was a doorway with no door in it. It was very dark inside the doorway. Rhodes shined his light inside. There were steps leading down into the cellar. They didn't look any safer than the ones leading up to the second floor; if anything, they looked even more treacherous.

There was no stair rail at all, not attached to the steps. It had fallen off, and Rhodes thought he could see what was left of it lying on the stone cellar floor down below. The right side of the stairway was unprotected.

The steps themselves did not inspire Rhodes with a spirit of adventure. Mainly they made him want to look for another way to get into the cellar. He thought that there was probably an outside entrance, but he didn't know that for sure. He might as well give this one a try. He couldn't tell with certainty, but it looked as if someone had made the trip only recently, and he could do it if they could.

He started down.

He walked as close to the wall as he could, going on the theory that if the wood was rotten it would break in the middle, which would be the weak point of the boards. He shined his light in front of him as he went.

There were two broken steps in a row, about halfway down. Rhodes stretched his legs and stepped over them, leaning into the wall. The next step took his weight and held, but it creaked loudly. When he pulled away from the wall, he could feel spider webs peeling off along with him.

The creaking step had eliminated the element of surprise, he thought, not that there was much chance of catching anyone unaware after driving into the yard and slamming the car door. He wasn't trying to startle anyone, anyhow. He didn't want the twins, if they were there, to think he was dangerous. That might scare them, and scared people were sometimes more hazardous to one's health than people who were more or less relaxed.

The cellar was dark as a dungeon, and the air was dank, or that's the way Rhodes thought of it. He didn't have much experience with dankness, not having spent much time in dark, cool, humid environments. There was a damp, musty smell in the air.

His right arm brushed the dense coating of cobwebs on the wall as he descended, and he stopped to wipe them off his shirt, along with the ones he had accumulated when he leaned against the wall. They stuck to his hand and he shook it hard. The cobwebs drifted to the steps.

He went on down, testing each step with his foot before putting his full weight down on it. He wondered if he would be as worried about breaking through if he had exercised regularly on the stationary bicycle and lost a few pounds. He decided that he probably would be.

He reached the bottom of the stairs without incident. Standing on the solid stone floor, he looked around with the help of the light.

He was in a small stone-walled room about eight feet by ten. There was a doorway across the room in front of him and another in the wall to his left. Evidently the cellar was divided into several rooms. He wondered just which one of them Mr. Findley was supposed to have been chopped up in.

There was a faint light in the room to his left, and Rhodes assumed that it was coming from the outside.

He shined the light down at the floor. It was dirty, but the dirt had been scuffed around. He didn't see any ninety-year-old bloodstains.

"Anybody here?" he called. "Claude? Clyde? This is Sheriff Rhodes. I want to talk to you." His voice echoed hollowly from the stone walls.

There was no answer to his call, but then he hadn't really expected one.

"I'll wait right here by the stairs for a minute. Why don't you two come in here where we can talk?"

There was still no answer. Rhodes listened closely, but he could hear no movement in the other areas of the cellar. Maybe he had been wrong. Maybe Claude and Clyde weren't down there after all.

He counted to sixty twice and was about to move into the next room when he heard something in there scrape against the stone floor.

It might have been a rat, but then again it might have been something else. He waited for another minute, but the sound was not repeated.

"Claude? Clyde? Is that you? I just want to talk. Your daddy's in jail, but your mother and sister are all right. You can see them later if you come with me."

The twins, if they were there, weren't talking. Rhodes was going to have to go looking for them.

He decided to try the room with light coming in, not that there was much light at this time of day. That room was where the sound had come from, however, and if he were hiding out in a cellar, he wouldn't want to be in complete darkness.

The part he didn't like was going through the doorway.

He'd seen it done in the movies often enough, heroic cops getting a running start and lunging through the door in a forward roll, coming up with their .44 Magnums blazing, but he didn't want to shoot anyone, and besides, he was holding a flashlight that he didn't want to drop.

The fact that he didn't think he could do a forward roll on a stone floor, or any other kind of floor for that matter, entered into it, too.

He stepped to within a foot of the door and shined the light inside. There was nothing he could see there but stone walls and spider webs. There was a small rectangular window on the wall opposite the door. The last of the late afternoon light leaked through it.

Rhodes extended his arm, pushing the flashlight through the doorway.

Something came out of the darkness to his right and smashed into the light, sending it crashing to the floor. The lens cracked on the stone and the halogen bulb shattered. The light went out.

Rhodes was through the door and across the room almost by the time the light hit the floor. He hadn't known for sure he could move that fast, but he was glad to see that he could. No forward roll, though.

He didn't have a .44 Magnum, but his short-barreled .38 Police Special was in his hand and he was pointing it at the two dark forms that hulked against the opposite wall on either side of the doorway. One of them was holding something that looked like a three-foot length of two-by-four.

"You boys are mighty hard to find," Rhodes said.

The one with the two-by-four took a step forward.

"You better stay where you are and put that thing down, Claude," Rhodes said. "Or Clyde."

"You gonna make me?" the twin said.

Good grief, Rhodes thought. He wished people would come up with some new way of making conversation with him.

"Yes," he said. "If I have to."

Claude, or Clyde, hesitated longer than Rhodes liked, but then he tossed the plank to the floor. It clattered against the stone, bounced, and lay still.

"Is there another way out of here besides those front stairs?" Rhodes said.

The twin who had thrown down the plank said, "No."

"Well, what do you say we go up those stairs and have our little talk, then," Rhodes said. "This place is getting on my nerves. You two can go first."

The twins didn't seem to like his suggestion, but after looking at each other briefly they turned and went through the doorway.

Rhodes followed them. "Go on up," he said when they got to the stairs. "One at a time, and be careful. It's dark in here. You go first, Claude."

He didn't have any idea which one was Claude, but he didn't think it mattered.

One of the twins started up the stairs.

"Stick close to the wall," Rhodes said to the dark shape.

When the first twin reached the second step, Rhodes said, "Now you, Clyde," and the second twin followed.

Rhodes was close behind. They didn't get far.

Clyde broke through the third step, which divided with a loud snap beneath his foot. As he was falling, he reached up and grabbed Claude's pants at the waist, dragging Claude down on top of him. Both of them fell backward into Rhodes, who didn't have time to get out of the way.

They all hit the stairs together and went crashing through the bottom step. Dirt, dust, and cobwebs filled the air. Rhodes could hear one of the twins sneezing as he tried to get out from under them, and then they were wrestling him, trying to wrench the pistol from his hand.

He refused to let go, and as the gun was yanked this way and that, he was afraid someone would get shot.

He selfishly hoped it wouldn't be him.

Just as he was thinking about it, one of the twins gave an extra hard jerk, and Rhodes inadvertently triggered off a shot. Red and blue flames leapt from the barrel of the pistol, and the bullet spanged off first one wall and then another before it buried itself in some part of the remaining stairway. The noise of the shot was extremely loud in the stone-walled room, and the echoes seemed to go on forever.

The shot scared Rhodes, but it scared the twins even more. One of them jumped up and was yelling, "I'm blind! I'm blind!" over and over, while the other one, still lying on top of Rhodes, yelled, "Claude! Claude! Are you all right?"

Or that was what Rhodes thought the boy yelled. His ears were ringing, and he couldn't be sure.

Rhodes shoved himself from beneath the remaining twin, Clyde, and got to his feet. Both twins continued to yell, and Rhodes wished that he had his police whistle with him. He was tempted to fire the pistol again just to get their attention, but he didn't.

He waited for a minute until they had calmed down a bit and then said, "You aren't blind, Claude." His voice sounded both dim and hollow at the same time. "You were just looking a little too closely at the muzzle flash. You should have closed your eyes, but you'll be all right after a while. You're just lucky you didn't get your eye shot out, pulling a stupid stunt like that."

"He didn't pull nothin'!" Clyde said, still agitated. "It was an accident!"

"He was trying to take the pistol away from me," Rhodes said. "That was no accident."

"I meant fallin' was an accident," Clyde said. "He didn't mean to."

"He meant to try for the gun," Rhodes said. "It wasn't a good idea."

"You didn't have to blind me!" Claude yelled. "And I'm nearly deaf, too!"

"Listen to me," Rhodes said. "You aren't blind. Can you hear that?"

"I can hear you! But I can't see!"

"You'll be able to see soon enough. Now be quiet."

Claude sniffled a time or two, and then he was quiet.

"You don't have to be so rough on him," Clyde said. "He didn't mean nothin'."

Rhodes wasn't going to get into that again. He wished his ears would stop ringing, and he wished he could see the stairs better, but it was almost dark outside now and it was even darker in the cellar. It was too bad about the broken flashlight.

"We're going to try it again," he said. "This time, Clyde, you go first. Claude, you go right behind him, with your hand on his belt. You'll have to tell him where to step, Clyde."

"I can't see," Claude said.

"We get the idea," Rhodes said. "Take his hand, Clyde. Get him started. Feel along the wall, and you can make it." He hoped he wasn't lying.

As it turned out, he wasn't. They made it to the top that time without incident, even with all the broken steps. It took them five full minutes, with much complaining by Claude that he couldn't see and couldn't hear and couldn't find the steps with his foot and that he was going to fall and break his neck.

Rhodes was willing to break it first, but eventually Clyde got his brother to hush and they finally got back to the first floor.

"Now let's go out on the porch," Rhodes told them. "I have a few questions to ask you."

"I can't see," Claude said.

"Help your brother," Rhodes told Clyde, who guided his twin down the hallway and out the door.

"You gonna read us our rights?" Clyde said when they

reached the front porch. "On TV, they always read 'em their rights."

Rhodes didn't have to read, since he knew the Miranda warning by heart, and it was too dark for reading in the first place, but he got out the card anyway.

Anything to make sure that life was like TV said it was supposed to be. He didn't want to disappoint the customers.

15

▼

IT WAS QUIET ON THE PORCH, AND THE SLIGHT EVENING breeze was a welcome change from the dank air of the basement. Rhodes could smell the cedars, and he could see, off down the road, the lights in the nearest house. He wondered if the people who lived there were eating supper. He wondered if Ivy was thinking about him, and he hoped she didn't mind, too much, that he wasn't there again.

The twins didn't want to say anything, even after having their rights read to them, except that Claude needed a doctor for his eyes. And that he still couldn't hear well.

Rhodes couldn't hear too well, either, for that matter, but he persuaded the twins that they would be better off if they just answered a few questions right there. Otherwise, they would have to answer them in the jail, where the atmosphere was much less pleasant.

"Well, all right," Clyde said. "Ask something."

Now that he had the chance to ask, Rhodes didn't know where to start. He decided that Graham's death was as good a place as any, but he wanted to work up to it gradually. He'd get to Miz Coates after they talked about Graham.

"How long had you two been working at the college for Mr. Graham?" he said.

"Off and on, ever since we moved to Obert, I guess," Clyde said. "Wouldn't nobody else give us a job, on account of they didn't like our daddy, but Mr. Graham, he didn't care about things like that."

"Like what?" Rhodes said.

Neither of the twins responded.

Rhodes waited quietly for a full minute. Then he said, "I asked you a question."

"I can't see a thing," Claude said. "You blinded me with that pistol."

Rhodes didn't feel like telling him again that he wouldn't be permanently sightless or that it was Claude's own fault that the gun had gone off in his face. So he didn't say anything at all. He just stood there looking up through the cedar trees to catch a glimpse of the evening stars that were beginning to show in the dark sky. They were clear and brilliant, almost white. There was a cricket singing somewhere nearby.

Finally Clyde said, "Folks say our daddy's an outlaw. They say we steal stuff."

"What folks?" Rhodes said.

"Like that Miz Coates. She's called the Laws on us before."

"And do you steal things?" Rhodes said. He didn't have to ask about their father. He was already convinced that Appleby was an outlaw.

"You told us that everything we say can be used against us, didn't you?" Clyde said.

"That's right," Rhodes said. "I did."

"Then we didn't steal nothin'." The falsity of the statement was almost palpable in the darkness of the early evening.

"It won't do you any good to lie," Rhodes said. "I've

already got a warrant to search your house. Whatever's there I'll find it."

"We sold ever'thing already," Clyde said.

Claude kicked him in the ankle. "You dumb shit," he said.

"There are worse things than stealing," Rhodes said, thinking about Miz Coates and what Clyde had said about her calling the Laws.

"What'd'you mean?" Clyde said. "About things bein' worse."

"Murder," Rhodes said. "For one thing."

"We didn't kill Mr. Graham," Claude said, surprising Rhodes. "We might've took things, but we never killed him."

"What about Miz Coates?" Rhodes said. "You don't seem to have liked her much. Did you kill her?"

"You tryin' to fool with us?" Clyde said. "Like they do on TV?"

"I'm not trying to fool with you," Rhodes said.

"Well, you must be. Miz Coates ain't dead."

Rhodes couldn't see Clyde's face well at all. It was too dark on the porch for that. But it would be hard for anyone who knew Miz Coates was dead, much less the person who had killed her, to sound so convincing.

"She's dead, all right," Rhodes said. "Someone killed her this afternoon."

The twins thought about that.

Claude said, "Well, I can't say we're sorry. She never did treat us right. But we didn't kill her. We been right here, ever since you come to the house looking for our daddy."

"Can you prove it?" Rhodes said.

"Sure," Claude said. "Clyde, he can tell you I was here. And I can tell you *he* was here. We got an alibi."

"That's right," Clyde said. "An alibi."

Rhodes didn't bother telling them what he thought about

their alibiing one another. "Why did you think that you had to hide out?" he said.

"We didn't want you gettin' after us because of stealin' them—" Claude said. He was cut off in mid-sentence by Clyde, who jammed an elbow into his ribs.

"That's all right, Clyde," Rhodes said. "I already had you two figured for helping with the cows. Your daddy couldn't have done it by himself."

"We don't know nothin' about any cows," Clyde said. "Do we, Claude."

"Hell no," Claude said. "All I know is, I've been blinded. I'm gonna sue for police brutality."

Rhodes started to tell the young man that the Sheriff's Department had already been sued by experts and that the experts had lost, but he thought better of it. And he wasn't interested in talking about the cows right now. The cows were the least of his worries. He could get back to the cows some other time, though, if the blood testing didn't prove what he hoped it would prove.

"And you haven't left this house all day?" Rhodes said, ignoring Claude.

"That's right," Clyde said. "We sure ain't."

"All right, then," Rhodes said. "Let's go to jail."

He wasn't at all satisfied with the way things were turning out. It was obvious that Cy Appleby couldn't have killed Oma Coates. He had been in jail at the time of her death. And now he didn't think Clyde and Claude were guilty, either. Which made it all the more important to find Hal Brame and discuss the discrepancies in his story. Miz Coates had seen his car the night Graham was killed, and Rhodes wished more than ever that he had pressed her and tried to make her tell him whatever she was holding back.

"What's the charges?" Claude said.

"We'll start with assaulting a police officer and work

from there," Rhodes said. "Cattle theft is a possibility we can consider, too."

"We don't know nothin' about those cows," Clyde said. "And we didn't know it was an officer we was assaultin' in the basement. It was dark down there."

Rhodes nodded in agreement. "That's what I'd say, too, if I were you," he told the twins. "It might even work. But it won't keep you out of jail."

He urged the twins off the porch and started them toward the car, Clyde leading his brother along. When they got to the car, Clyde turned around and faced Rhodes.

"Maybe we could make a trade," he said.

Everybody watches too much TV, Rhodes thought, not including himself in that number. After all, he watched mostly old movies; that didn't really count.

"I don't make trades," he said. He meant it. He was pretty sure that the twins hadn't told all they knew about things, the cattle theft being the least of the things they knew about, but he wasn't going to let them go free just for giving him information. He was sure they would tell him what they knew sooner or later.

"We're juveniles," Clyde said. "You can't do anything to us anyhow."

The fact that Clyde had a point didn't make Rhodes feel any better.

He opened the back door of the car. "Get in," he said. "Watch your heads."

"I can't see," Claude said.

"Don't worry," Rhodes told him. "I'll help you." He put his hand on Claude's head and guided him into the back seat. Then he got in the front and drove them to Clearview.

"James Allen called," Hack said after the twins were booked and Lawton was putting them into a cell next to their father. "He didn't sound real happy."

Allen was an old friend of Rhodes. He was also a county

commissioner, and Rhodes was sure he must have heard Red Rogers' news broadcast.

"Did he say what he wanted?" Rhodes said.

"Nope," Hack said. "He didn't sound like he was callin' just to see how you were doin', though. I told him you were on a hot case and maybe you could call him tomorrow."

"What did he say about that?"

"He said he hoped that hot case was the one from out at Obert. Said he hoped he could count on you havin' it solved by tomorrow when you called him."

"Is that all?"

"Nope. He said he thought maybe we'd need the Rangers on this one. It's gettin' too big for us small-town boys."

Rhodes hoped Allen was wrong about that, but with two murders in two days the Rangers would be getting interested whether Rhodes wanted them to or not.

The radio crackled, and Hack responded. It was Ruth Grady, reporting that she'd found an abandoned car.

"Gimme the license number," Hack said. He wrote down the number. "Got it. The sheriff's right here. I'll send him on out." He listened a little longer. Rhodes could make out Ruth's description of an automobile and its location. "Right," Hack said. "A black Volvo. Got it." He signed off and turned to his computer.

"You don't need that," Rhodes said. "I think I know who that car belongs to. Hal Brame."

"Thinkin's one thing," Hack said. "Knowin's another. And I'll tell you somethin' else. If we had portable computers in all the patrol cars, Ruth coulda done the checkin' herself. I think we oughta—"

"Don't start," Rhodes said. "We're lucky to have what we've got."

"All the same, I wish you'd talk to the commissioners about gettin' computers for all the cars. It'd save a world of time and bother."

"It would save a world of time if you'd just enter that license number right now," Rhodes said.

Hack looked hurt, but he typed the license number into his computer. He watched the information come up on the monitor screen.

"Name's Henry, not Hal," he said. "That Hal part, that must be a nickname. But you were right about the owner, sure enough. I guess you're right about the computers, too. I guess we don't really need computers long as we got a hotshot lawman like you around. All you gotta do is hear the make of the car and then you know all about who it belongs to. I guess—"

"All right," Rhodes said. "I get the point. Are you going to tell me where the car is, or not?"

"Huh?" Hack said. "You mean to tell me you don't already know? I'd figure you could tell *me,* you bein' so good at stuff like that."

"Hack," Rhodes said.

"Out east of Gorton," Hack said. "Take a left on that gravel road that goes to that wooden bridge over Little Man Creek. It's down in the creek by the bridge."

"Was there anyone in it?"

"Not that Ruth saw. She was gonna wait on you to make a complete search."

"Will we need a wrecker?"

"She says yes. It's partly in the water. Creek's up a little bit now, what with all the rain we got in the Easter spell."

"I'd better call Ivy," Rhodes said.

"I'd say that might be a good idea," Hack said. "I expect it's gonna be a long night."

Rhodes didn't know how Little Man Creek had gotten its name. In actuality it was hardly a creek at all; generally it was more like a trickle, and often during especially dry summers it wasn't even that. At some time in the distant past, however, it must have been a fast-moving stream, since it had cut a deep ravine through the landscape, thus necessitating the bridge that now spanned it.

The road down which Rhodes traveled to reach the bridge did not see much traffic these days. There were only a few farm houses left along it, and several of these were deserted. At one time Blacklin County had been one of the largest producers of cotton in the state, but hardly anyone grew cotton now, or anything else. Most of the land that had once been farmed was used for grazing cattle or for nothing at all. There were quite a few nearly deserted roads like this one in the county. You could travel along them for miles without meeting a car or seeing anyone.

Ruth had been patrolling it only because of the current situation in Obert. Rhodes had told her to make a thorough sweep through that part of the county. Even at that, as she explained to him when he arrived at the bridge, she had seen the car only by accident. She had noticed that the weeds in the bar ditch were broken and flat, and then one of her headlights had glinted off the back bumper of the Volvo, so she had stopped to investigate.

"Have you checked it out?" Rhodes said. They were standing at one end of the bridge, looking down. Ruth had parked nearby and had her car's spotlight trained on the car.

"No," Ruth said. "I can see something in the front seat, though. Can you?"

Rhodes wasn't sure. There might be something, or someone, in there, but it was hard to tell. The spotlight was creating quite a few shadows in addition to casting light.

"Anyway," Ruth said, "I thought I'd better wait until you got here before I went down there. I didn't want to slip and fall in the creek."

"Good idea," Rhodes said.

The sloping bank was steep, and the weeds might hide treacherous footing. They might also hide snakes. Although Rhodes had never seen a rattlesnake in the county, he had seen cottonmouth water moccasins. There wasn't much to choose between them and rattlesnakes when you got right down to it. In fact, a cottonmouth might be the meaner of the two.

He was going to say that they could wait for the wrecker, but he knew that he should go down to the car. There was always the chance that there was something to be found, and the wrecker driver would need help hooking on to the car.

"I'll go on down now," Ruth said.

"I'll go," Rhodes told her. It wasn't that Ruth was a woman. He just thought that it was his job to do. He was the sheriff. He took his flashlight and started down the slope, hanging on to some of the taller and tougher weeds to keep himself from sliding too fast.

He didn't fall, and he didn't encounter any snakes. The car rested at the bottom of the creek bank, nose down into the sluggish water that showed up black in the spotlight. Only the Volvo's front bumper and grille were in the creek. Most of the car was high and dry.

Just as he got to the back of the car Rhodes slipped and almost fell. He braced himself on the car trunk and told himself that what he saw in the front seat had not caused his near-fall.

What he saw was a person, or at least the head of one, resting against the car's steering wheel.

Rhodes steadied himself and moved carefully to the front door on the driver's side. He shined his light in through the closed window and into the dead face of Hal Brame. Brame's eyes were open and it was almost as if he were looking at something very interesting on the steering column. Brame hadn't been wearing a seat belt.

Rhodes didn't climb back up the bank immediately. He knew the wrecker would arrive soon, and it did. The driver climbed down and with a little help from Rhodes got hooked on to the Volvo. Before long he had pulled it to the road. Rhodes climbed back up after it.

"You want me to haul it to the jail?" the driver said.

"Not yet," Rhodes said. "We'll have to call a justice of the peace. There's a dead man in there."

"Right," the driver said. He wasn't surprised at the mention of the dead man, and he didn't seem to mind waiting, despite the lateness of the hour. The county was paying him good money.

Rhodes radioed Hack and told him to send the EMS unit and the J.P.

"I looked around up here," Ruth said. She pointed her flashlight to the other side of the road. "You can tell that a car backed into the weeds over there, but you can't tell whether it was the Volvo or another one."

Rhodes looked at the mashed weeds. There could have been another car, all right. It could have pulled onto the bridge, then backed around and turned toward Gorton. The weeds were too thick for the car to have left any tire impressions on the edge of the ditch, however.

The fact that another car had been there didn't mean much, though Rhodes was already beginning to wonder if Brame's death was an accident.

He thought about the possibilities. If it was an accident, why here? What would Brame have been doing in this part of the county? There was nothing here to interest him.

Then there was the possibility of suicide. Brame, if he was guilty of killing Graham and Oma Coates, had been unable to live with the knowledge and had driven off the road deliberately.

Well, it was possible, but Brame could have found a much better place for suicide. He would have been much more likely just to get a few bruises than to kill himself at this spot. Rhodes was certain that it was murder.

It took a while for things to get squared away, but finally the J.P. declared Brame dead and his body was taken away in the ambulance. The wrecker chugged off down the road, towing the Volvo behind.

"Let's go on back to town," Rhodes told Ruth Grady. "You can go over the car for prints, and we'll see if we can find anything helpful in it."

Ruth didn't want to risk getting stuck in the ditch. She drove across the bridge and went on until she came to a side road that furnished her with a better place to turn around. Rhodes followed her and turned at the same spot. He didn't want to get stuck, either.

The wrecker driver dropped the Volvo at the jail, and Rhodes searched it thoroughly after Ruth had lifted what prints she could. It seemed as if he were searching a lot of abandoned property lately.

He didn't find anything inside that was of any use to him. There were some book catalogs, a road map, a quart-sized insulated plastic drink cup with a top so that the contents wouldn't spill, a box of Kleenex tissues, and an owner's manual. The manual told him that he was dealing with a 1984 Volvo DL, but that hardly seemed relevant to the murder. There was a battered leather suitcase in the trunk, filled with clothing and toiletries.

There was no sign of anything that looked like *Tamerlane*. That didn't surprise Rhodes at all.

16

▼

RHODES GOT HOME VERY LATE. HE GOT HOLD OF DR. WHITE and arranged for him to have a look at Brame's body as soon as he could, got the body taken care of by Ballinger's, instructed Hack to make a few phone calls as early as he could the next morning, and finally got away from the jail a little before two o'clock.

Ivy was watching *Fort Apache* when Rhodes walked in.

"It must be John Wayne week," Rhodes said.

"It is," Ivy said. She was sitting on the couch, her feet tucked up under her. "Tomorrow night, they're showing *The Searchers.*"

Rhodes watched a few minutes of the movie. He thought John Agar was almost as good in this one as he was in *The Brain from Planet Arous.* But not quite.

"I wish you wouldn't stay up so late waiting for me," he said. "It makes me feel guilty."

"Who said I was waiting for you?"

"Well, I just thought—"

"Are there any beautiful women involved in this case?" Ivy said.

Rhodes thought about Marty Wallace. "I guess you could say that there was one."

"Then maybe I *want* you to feel guilty," Ivy said. "Did you ever think of that?"

"No," Rhodes said. "It doesn't seem like you."

"You never know." Ivy uncurled herself and stood up. "Did you eat any supper?"

"I forgot again."

"It's not good for you to forget things like that. Come on in the kitchen."

Rhodes followed her to the kitchen. There was no more meat loaf, but this time there was cold roast beef.

"It would have been warm roast beef if you'd come home by ten o'clock," Ivy said. "After you called, I gave up on you and put it in the refrigerator."

"I'm sorry," Rhodes said. "It's not going to be this way all the time. I promise. We don't have that many murders around here."

He went on to tell her the whole story about Oma Coates, his search for the Appleby twins, the discovery of Brame's body in the Volvo.

"How are Mrs. Appleby and Twyla Faye?" he asked, helping himself to a thick slice of the roast. It would make as good a sandwich as the meat loaf, or even better. He noticed that it was a very lean roast and that Ivy had cut off all the fat when she sliced it. He spread two pieces of the oat bran bread with the light salad dressing and mustard.

"They're fine," Ivy said. "I think both of them are ready to get some counseling. Neither one of them will testify against the husband, but neither one seems sorry that you arrested him. I told them that you might be able to send him to prison for cattle theft even without their testimony, and they didn't seem very sorry about that, either."

"Good," Rhodes said, after making his sandwich and taking a bite. It was as good as he'd thought it would be, even if he did have to use the oat bran bread.

He told Ivy about Brame's murder then and wondered aloud if there were some way he might be able to tie Appleby to it, but he didn't think so. The twins, however, were a different story.

"I know they're not telling me everything," he told Ivy. "Oma Coates knew more than she was telling, too. If people would just talk to me, we could get this taken care of."

"It seems to me there aren't that many suspects left," Ivy said.

"I'm not counting the twins out of it, yet," Rhodes said. "I don't think they killed Oma Coates, but they seemed to know that Graham had been murdered. They talked as if they liked him, but that doesn't mean a thing, not if they thought big money was involved." He told Ivy how much the *Tamerlane* might be worth. "They could have killed Brame, too," he added.

"Why?" Ivy said.

"I haven't worked that part out yet." Rhodes got up and got himself a Dr Pepper to wash down the sandwich. "It might be that he found the book, though, and they killed him for that."

"I'd think they were the kind to take things if they killed someone, all right," Ivy said. "They wouldn't just go off and leave the car, though."

Rhodes got his Dr Pepper and took a swallow. "They know cars are easy to trace," he said. "And that Volvo would stand out like a jet airplane around here."

"Even if they left the car because of that, they wouldn't leave an unopened suitcase."

"They might if they were in a hurry and didn't search the trunk," Rhodes said.

"So what does all this leave you with?" Ivy said.

"It leaves me with a theory or two, but nothing that I can arrest anybody with. Not yet, anyway."

"That's too bad. I heard Red Rogers today."

"Me too. I can't wait until tomorrow, when he'll have Hal Brame's corpse to talk about. Sometimes I think he wants to get me in a recall election."

Ivy didn't think so. "He just wants to get as many people to listen to him as he can. But I think you might have a lot more of the media people from Dallas and Houston coming around again when they find out that Brame's been murdered. No one's going to believe that Graham committed suicide now, not after all this."

Rhodes knew she was right. Thinking about it, he didn't sleep very well at all that night.

It was nearly nine o'clock when he got to the jail the next morning. Hack and Lawton smirked when he came in, but they didn't say anything at first.

Hack couldn't resist for long, however. "You know somethin', Lawton?" he said.

Lawton said he didn't know much of anything.

Hack was pleased to enlighten him. "It seems to me that when a fella gets married it does somethin' to his whatchamacallit. His metabolism. Slows it down somethin' awful. You take a man who used to be able to get to work at the crack of dawn, well, he might not get in till eight o'clock. Eight-thirty, maybe. Sometimes, nine o'clock. It's terrible to see a fella slow down like that."

Rhodes would not be baited. "Are the twins awake yet?" he said.

"Sure are," Lawton told him. "You take a couple of young boys like that, they don't need as much sleep as an old man might, 'specially if the old man's got him a new wife at home. They been up for hours."

Rhodes didn't let Lawton bother him any more than Hack had. He said, "I think I'll go up and have a word with them."

"Mind those stairs, you hear?" Hack said. "They might be a little tricky for a fella in your condition."

Rhodes went through the door without a word.

He heard Lawton say, "Reckon he's gettin' hard of hearin', too?" as the door closed.

* * *

The twins were sitting on the edges of their bunks, smoking cigarettes and talking to their father in the next cell when Rhodes entered the cellblock. They got very quiet when he came in.

The flasher was in the cell across from Appleby. He was either still asleep or pretending to be. Rhodes didn't blame him. It most likely wouldn't be a good idea to overhear a conversation among members of the Appleby family.

"You come to spring us, Sheriff?" Appleby said.

"No," Rhodes said. "I don't think you'll be getting out anytime soon."

"I can plead self-defense. You threatened me."

"It's not the assault that you ought to be worried about," Rhodes said. "It's the cattle."

Appleby laughed. "I got the bill of sale."

"We'll see," Rhodes said. He hoped that lab report came in soon. "I want to talk to your sons."

"They don't want to talk to you," Appleby said. "Do you, boys?"

"Nah," Clyde said.

Rhodes looked at the other twin. "How are your eyes today, Claude?"

"I can see all right."

"Good. Now then, last night you said something about a trade. What did you want to trade me?"

"Nothin'," Clyde said. "And you said you didn't make trades."

"I told you they didn't want to talk," Appleby said.

"It might be easier for them if they did."

"Easier for you, you mean," Appleby said, sitting on his bunk and leaning back against the stone wall of the cell with his hands crossed behind his head. Rhodes really didn't like the man.

"Easier for all of us is what I meant," Rhodes said. "But I can do it the hard way if I have to."

"You might as well do it, then," Appleby said. "You won't get nothin' from one of us."

Rhodes didn't bother to say any more. He had thought a lot about things after going to bed the previous night, which was one reason he had been late getting to the jail, and he was convinced that he had put everything together, more or less. What he lacked was proof, and it would have been better if he could have gotten some help from the twins. He thought he might, eventually. Their father might be accustomed to being in jail, but they weren't.

Besides, he had lied to them. He had decided that he was willing to make a trade, but not until there was no other choice.

He didn't see any real point in sending the twins to the juvenile version of prison until he was certain of their crimes, however, so he was willing to let things rock along as they were for a little longer.

When Rhodes left the cellblock, the flasher was still feigning sleep.

He went back down to the office, where Hack and Lawton were contriving to look busy.

"Did you make those phone calls that I asked you about last night?" he said.

"I sure did," Hack said. "You were right." He looked over at Lawton, who had his broom and was beginning to sweep up. "But then we shoulda known that. You don't even need the computer to figure things out. You—"

"Hack," Rhodes said.

"Huh?"

"Can they give us a positive I.D.?"

"Sure. All we gotta do is trot out the suspects or show 'em a picture. They're pretty sure."

"Where did you locate them?"

"They didn't go far, like you thought. Gorton."

"We'll need the telephone records."

Hack looked pleased with himself. "I thought about that. Shouldn't be any trouble. All that stuff's on computer these days."

"Good. What about the Lakeway Inn?"

"Same deal. You were right about that, too."

"Even better. Now call Dr. Slick and see if he's found out anything about those blood samples."

Hack got on the phone and called the veterinarian. "He wants to talk to you," he told Rhodes after a few seconds' conversation.

Rhodes got on his extension. "What have you got for me?" he said.

"It's what you've got that matters," Slick said. "I think you've got a case."

"Good," Rhodes said. He meant it sincerely. "Tell me."

"There's a good chance that the bull we sampled is the sire of those calves."

"How good?" Rhodes said.

"Real good. We took blood from four calves, and they all match up with that Santa Gertrudis. The odds against getting that kind of a match on four out of four are so high that the lab guys didn't even try to compute them."

"That's good, all right," Rhodes said, wondering if Appleby would be quite so relaxed up there in his cell if he knew that there was a really strong case building against him. "I just hope the jury we get will agree. You'll testify at the trial if we need you, won't you?"

"Sure. And the jury will agree, don't worry about that. The odds are up in the billions if not more."

"Great," Rhodes said.

"There's just one thing," Slick said.

"What's that?"

"If we ever do this again, I hope the next guy you pick won't be so easy to rile as this one was. He might jump me instead of you."

"Don't worry about that," Rhodes said. "I'll protect you. And thanks."

"No problem," Slick said. "It was almost fun, especially the mud wrestling."

"Don't remind me," Rhodes said. He hung up and told Hack to call Dr. White, who confirmed Rhodes's suspicions about Brame's "accident."

There hadn't been an accident at Little Man Creek at all, and there had been no suicide. Brame had been strangled, not unlike Oma Coates, though of course there was no way to prove that it had been done by the same person. Someone had pushed his car into the creek, maybe hoping that no one would investigate further. Or maybe not having a very high opinion of the law officers of Blacklin County.

Rhodes thanked Dr. White and asked Hack to call Adkins. "And tell him to get down here. I want to talk to him."

Hack was already dialing.

Adkins was glad to know that he was going to get his cattle back, but he wasn't entirely pleased with the lecture Rhodes gave him.

"In the first place, this was expensive for the county," Rhodes said, explaining that the vet and the lab didn't work for free. "It's going to cost us around five hundred dollars."

"Those cows are worth that much," Adkins said. "They're worth a lot more."

"To you," Rhodes said.

"But you're gettin' a cattle thief off the streets," Adkins said. "That's worth somethin'."

"He didn't steal the cattle on the streets," Rhodes said. He couldn't resist.

"Well, you know what I mean," Adkins said.

Rhodes knew. "But if you'd branded those cattle, we wouldn't have had this problem. They probably wouldn't have been stolen in the first place."

"You sayin' I encouraged him?"

"Not exactly. But you didn't do anything to *dis*courage him."

"I'll brand 'em from now on," Adkins said.

He refused to meet the sheriff's eyes, and Rhodes knew that Adkins wouldn't follow through. Adkins was like a lot of people Rhodes had talked to since becoming sheriff; they always took the easy way, no matter how much trouble it caused anyone else. In a way, Appleby and Adkins had more in common than Adkins would ever have admitted. Appleby took the easy way, too.

"Another thing," Rhodes said. "If you'd had a bull and if someone had stolen it along with the rest of your herd, we might not have been able to do the blood tests. You would never have gotten those cattle back."

Adkins was still looking at the floor. "I ain't got no bull, though."

"Right," Rhodes said. His lecture wasn't getting him anywhere. He almost regretted that he'd spotted Adkins's cows in that pasture.

But then he thought about what else he had learned about Appleby, and he was no longer regretful. Appleby wouldn't be hitting his wife again for a long time, if ever; and since his wife had refused to testify against him, the cattle theft charge was what would be keeping Appleby away from her. That fact was worth more than five hundred dollars and all of Adkins's cows lumped together.

"When can I have my cows back?" Adkins said.

"That might take a while," Rhodes said.

"But—"

"Don't worry about it. They're getting free grazing right now, anyway."

Adkins brightened. He hadn't thought of that. "Okay. But I want 'em as soon as I can have 'em."

"I'll let you know," Rhodes said.

Adkins left the jail in a fairly good mood.

"I bet he's on his way to the courthouse to register his

brand right now," Hack said. He had been listening to every word.

"Sure he is," Lawton said. "And then he'll have him a brandin' iron made."

"Count on it," Rhodes said. They all laughed.

17

▼

ON THE WAY TO OBERT ONE MORE TIME, RHODES LOOKED OUT at the last of the rusting oil derricks that could still be seen on the outskirts of Clearview, reminders of a time when the town had been on the boom and a much livelier spot than it now was, or livelier than it now was as a general thing. The last few days had been all too lively for Rhodes.

A few people had become very rich as a result of the oil days, and there were still some signs of their existence in Clearview. Their names were still prominent, and their homes were still the biggest in town.

But for most of the population, the boom had made little difference even at the time it was occurring, and it made even less difference now. Ancient history. Many of the derricks had remained standing for years, but most of them were gone now, sold for steel. Hardly anyone in town remembered the boom days; hardly anyone cared. The remaining derricks were the last reminder, and soon they would be gone, too.

It was funny how something like a little book, or pamphlet, whatever *Tamerlane* was, something made of paper, anyway, could outlast even those steel derricks and could cause so much trouble so many years after its publication.

If it was even real. Rhodes hadn't seen it yet, and he wasn't absolutely sure anyone else had. He thought someone had, though. All he had to do was prove it.

He parked his car outside the main building and walked up to the third floor where someone had killed Simon Graham.

It was hot and stuffy in the big room, but there was no one there. Marty Wallace and Mitch Rolingson were probably in the house. Their cars were there, at any rate.

Rhodes looked up at the beam where the rope had hung. Hal Brame could have taken the rope, dropped it over Graham's head, and hoisted Graham right up to the beam, or so Rhodes had thought for a while. Brame's size argued against that possibility, however. Graham was no giant, but hoisting him up that high would have required more strength than Brame seemed likely to have possessed.

Rhodes crossed over to the windows and looked out across the field to the pile of huge rocks. They looked even more like dinosaurs from a distance. Then he turned back to look at the rafters again.

Brame had been in this room, or nearby, when Graham was killed. Rhodes was convinced of that. There was no other way Brame could have heard the things he said he had heard. And Rhodes still thought Brame had deliberately called his attention to the body.

So who or what had Brame seen?

Appleby? It would have been no problem for Appleby to hang Graham. He had the build for it, and maybe even a motive, if hatefulness was a motive. But not the temperament. He would have used his bare hands, not set up a fake suicide.

Graham might have said something to the twins about the rapid building up of Appleby's cattle herd, and Appleby would have considered that meddlesome, just the way he considered Oma Coates meddlesome. But he did have a bill of sale for the cows, and he wouldn't have felt threatened enough to kill Graham over an offhand comment. He was vicious, but not that vicious. Or so Rhodes believed.

Rhodes let his gaze drop from the rafters and looked out the window. Two field larks—feelarks, Rhodes had called them when he was a kid; still did, for that matter—flew out of the grass as if they had been startled. They perched for a minute on top of the largest rock, and then they flew up and away. Rhodes lost sight of them in the intense blue of the sky.

His thoughts returned to Graham's murder. The twins were strong enough to hang two or three men, all at the same time, but Rhodes didn't think they had done it. They were hiding something, and he thought now that he knew what it was, but they weren't killers. They might even turn out to be all right if they got a chance to spend some time away from the influence of their father, and they were about to get that chance, thanks to the fact that the blood testing had worked out.

So as Ivy had said, that didn't leave very many suspects.

Only two. That narrowed the field, all right.

There was, however, the little matter of proof.

After finding Brame's body, Rhodes had asked Hack to call the local motels, as well as those in some of the sur- rounding counties.

He didn't really think Rolingson would have stayed right in Clearview, and he had been right about that. But the big man hadn't gone far, and the motel manager could identify him. So could the clerk at the Lakeway Inn. Brame hadn't checked out himself; Rolingson had checked him out. The night clerk had not been on duty when the checkout took place, and the day clerk had no idea that Rolingson wasn't Brame.

It was a good ploy, and it might even have worked if Rhodes hadn't caught on. It seemed clear that Rolingson didn't have a very high opinion of Rhodes's abilities.

But with the testimony of the clerk at the Lakeway Inn, Rhodes could tie Rolingson to Brame, though he didn't have anything that could be considered real proof that Rolingson was involved in killing anyone. Maybe Ruth would find Rolingson's prints in Brame's car.

As for hanging Graham, that would have been easy for the muscular Rolingson, as easy as it would have been for the equally powerful Appleby.

Rhodes left the window and went to the office door, which was still open. The place had been thoroughly searched, and toward the end the searching had become much less organized than it was at the beginning. Most of the books had not been replaced on the shelves, and it appeared that Rolingson and Wallace had been looking along the walls for a hidden safe or some other hiding place.

Why had Rolingson killed Graham? Rhodes still wasn't sure, but he was going to get in touch with Graham's lawyer as soon as he could and find out about Graham's will. He had a feeling that neither Wallace nor Rolingson would be mentioned in it, and that they both knew it. Rolingson would have wanted to get the book and get out, sell it quietly, maybe to Brame, and then deny ever having seen it.

So the book was one motive. Rhodes thought that Marty Wallace was another. She and Rolingson were almost blatantly living together now, and their relationship just as obviously was not a new one. Graham might not have approved; he might even have threatened to dissolve his partnership with Rolingson. Motives number two and three.

Now suppose that Brame had stumbled onto the murder by accident, having come to look at the Poe book. Suppose that he had gotten away before being spotted. He might have informed the sheriff in a roundabout way, to ensure his own safety, and then begun a little game of blackmail.

If that was the way things were, and Rhodes was pretty

sure he was right, or close to right, Brame had been fatally wrong about how well the sheriff could protect him.

So had Oma Coates, if she had even thought about it. Rhodes figured that she had seen something the night Graham died, too, probably Rolingson's car. Maybe she hadn't been certain about how it related to Graham's death, or maybe even she was interested in blackmail. Rhodes didn't know whether he would ever find out which was the case, but he was sure that Rolingson had killed her, as well.

There was the shotgun, for one thing. She had left it in the kitchen, or put it there. She had felt safe with whoever was in her house, had even walked back to the kitchen with him. She knew that Appleby was in jail, but she would surely have taken the gun and run the twins away from her door had they appeared there. But Rolingson? She might have had business to talk over with him, and the kitchen was the place for that.

It all came back to *Tamerlane*. When he'd first heard of it, Rhodes wouldn't have thought something like that could be a motive for murder. But when he'd talked to Scott and found out the book's true value to a collector, he had changed his mind. A quarter of a million dollars was more than enough to tempt almost anyone, especially if that someone were in financial trouble.

Still, why would Rolingson need to kill Graham? He was Graham's partner and would share in the proceeds if the book were sold, no matter who bought it.

That point had bothered Rhodes for a large part of the previous sleepless night, but then he thought about Marty Wallace and Rolingson's relationship to her. Graham had not even shown Rolingson the copy of *Tamerlane*, probably because he didn't trust him any longer. It was going to be Graham's book and Graham's sale. Rolingson had heard about it the same way others had, by rumor, and determined to do something to get the book for himself.

That was the how and the why of the murder, as best Rhodes could figure it.

Now all he had to do was prove it.

"What are you looking for, Sheriff?"

Rhodes twitched slightly at the sound of Marty Wallace's voice. He hadn't expected anyone to intrude on him, and he had been so deep in his thoughts that he hadn't heard her coming up the stairs.

"Clues," he said.

Marty Wallace laughed. She had a nice, throaty laugh; Rhodes thought it was too bad about her hairstyle. Too bad about her association with Rolingson, too.

"You won't find any clues in there," she said, smiling.

"How do you know?" Rhodes said. "There might be a thing or two you overlooked."

She stopped smiling. "I doubt that very much, Sheriff Rhodes."

Rhodes looked around the ransacked office again. "You're probably right. Where's your friend?"

"Mitch? He's over at the house. Why?"

"There are a few things I'd like to talk to him about," Rhodes said, leaving the office.

"I'll walk with you," Marty said.

The house didn't look like the same place, not on the inside. The almost antiseptic neatness had become near chaos. Floorboards had been pried up. Couch cushions had been slit open and the stuffing rearranged. Wallpaper had been peeled back.

"What happened?" Rhodes said when he entered the front door. "Did you have a burglary?"

Rolingson's voice came from somewhere in the back of the house. "Marty! Get your ass back here, now!"

Marty's face darkened at his tone, but she quickly forced a smile. "Mitch, why don't you come in the front room? We have company."

Rolingson came from the back bedroom. He was wearing a T-shirt that stretched its message across his chest. It said:

SEE DICK DRINK
SEE DICK DRIVE
SEE DICK DIE

Rhodes didn't have to see the back of the shirt to get the message, having seen similar shirts before. He knew that it said DON'T BE A DICK. More than the message, however, he was interested in Rolingson's arms, which the shirt showed to considerable advantage, and his hands. If John Henry had been built like that, the steam engine would have died instead of the steel-driving man. One of those hands could have encircled Oma Coates's thin neck, or Brame's.

"What do you want, Rhodes?" Rolingson's face was hard as rock; he seemed to have lost his grip on civility. That was no surprise to Rhodes. Rolingson had demonstrated even in their first conversation that he had a temper and that it wasn't always well controlled.

"I guess you haven't found the book yet," Rhodes said.

"That's none of your business. If you've got something important to say, say it. If you don't, why don't you just go on back to your sheriffing?"

Rhodes walked over to the vandalized couch, straightened the cushions and sat down. He looked across the room at Rolingson. "This little visit has to do with my sheriffing, as a matter of fact," he said.

Rolingson came to the couch and loomed over Rhodes. "Come on, then. If you have something to say, get it said. And then you can get out."

Rhodes looked up at Rolingson. He had heard that looming was supposed to give you an advantage in interviews, but he didn't think it worked that way when the loomer was as wrought up as Rolingson appeared to be.

"Why don't you and Miss Wallace have a seat?" Rhodes said. "This might take a while."

"I don't have time for a friendly chat, Sheriff," Rolingson said, not moving. "I'm a busy man."

Out of the corner of his eye, Rhodes could see that Marty was trying to get Rolingson to calm down by making discreet hand motions. It wasn't working.

"I don't have to be friendly if you don't want me to," Rhodes said. "We can start by talking about what you've done to this house. It isn't yours, and it looks to me like you've torn it up pretty good."

"Look," Rolingson said, trying to relax his tensed shoulders, "Miss Wallace and I have been through a damn tough time here. We've lost a good friend, and we just want to find what belongs to us and get out of this place."

"We haven't established that anything around here belongs to you," Rhodes said. "I'll be talking to Graham's lawyers about that little matter. Until then, you'd be better off if you stop looking for that book. I don't think you're going to find it, anyway."

Rolingson's head jerked, and he looked at Marty.

"Why not?" she said.

"Call it a hunch," Rhodes said. He crossed one leg over the other and leaned back on the couch.

"Hunch, my ass," Rolingson said, his mouth twisting into an ugly sneer. "I'm tired of your crap, Sheriff. Get up and get out of here."

"Mitch—" Marty Wallace said stepping over beside him and resting a hand on his huge left biceps.

"Shut up," Rollingson said, shaking her hand off. "This hick sheriff has been hassling us from the very beginning. That book's ours, and he can't do a damn thing about it. Isn't that right, hick?"

"Wrong," Rhodes said. "I can do a lot of things about it. For one thing, if it does turn up, I can impound it as evidence in a murder case."

"Murder?" Marty said. "But what does Ha—Simon's murder have to do with anything?"

"That depends," Rhodes said.

"Depends on what?" Rolingson said.

"On who told you Hal was murdered," Rhodes said, leaning forward on the couch so that he could get to his .38. He was pretty sure he couldn't take Rolingson barehanded.

"Stupid bitch," Rolingson said.

He didn't go for Rhodes. Instead, he reached out and grabbed Marty Wallace, his right hand encircling her arm. He jerked her toward him, snatched her off the floor, and threw her bodily at Rhodes.

Up until that instant, Rhodes had thought he was handling things exactly the right way. Rolingson seemed frazzled, in a bad mood, irritable. Typical of the man. Rhodes thought maybe he could stir him up, agitate him even more, and get him to blurt out something incriminating. Not that Rhodes had been trying that hard. He had been talking about Graham's murder, but Marty had interpreted his statement in the wrong way. Her preoccupation with Brame's murder had caused her to make a mistake.

Rhodes didn't think that even Red Rogers knew about Brame's death yet, so the only people who knew were those who had been on the scene the previous night—and the murderer, of course. Or, as Rhodes saw it now, the murderers.

He hadn't wanted to think that Marty Wallace was a party to the killings. She was too nearly beautiful to be a killer. He should have known better. He had already seen that she was greedy. And she had been in the motel with Rolingson; the records would show that she had checked her own messages, just as he had. She had been the one to calm Rolingson down and get him to go along with Brame earlier. How could she not have known that Brame had been murdered? Rhodes had a fleeting second to feel ashamed of himself for letting a pretty face so mislead him before she crashed into him.

Rolingson threw her hard. The front of her head and Rhodes's clonked together like two blocks of wood.

Rhodes fell back on the couch, and for a second he didn't see anything but blackness shot through with sparkling yellow and orange lights. His head felt at first as if it might float away from him. Then it started hurting like hell.

Marty bounced away from Rhodes, just missed the coffee table, and landed on the hardwood floor. Her head, the back of it this time, hit with a hard thunk.

Rhodes struggled against the waves of nausea that roiled up from his stomach and spun around in his head as he tried to get off the couch.

Rolingson kicked him in the chest. Rhodes shot back against the couch, and the couch slammed against the wall, stopping short and throwing Rhodes forward onto the floor. He caught himself on his hands, managing to avoid smashing his face into the wood. He held himself there, trying to focus on the floor, waiting for Rolingson's foot to punt his head through the window.

It wasn't that he *wanted* his head to be kicked through the window; it was just that he couldn't do anything to prevent its happening.

It didn't happen, however. Rolingson seemed to have decided to quit the premises. Through the throbbing that engulfed his head, Rhodes heard a door slam. Then he heard a car start and drive away.

Rhodes sat up, careful not to jar his head. He was afraid it might fall off if he did. He reached up and gingerly touched the spot on his forehead where he and Marty Wallace had collided. It was very tender, and a lump was beginning to form.

Even at that Rhodes was better off than Marty, who lay still as a stone on the floor nearby.

Rhodes put his hand to her neck, felt for a carotid artery.

There was a pulse, faint but regular. At least she wasn't dead. Rhodes didn't want to leave her there, but he felt an obligation to go after Rolingson.

Rhodes stood up shakily, putting a hand on the arm of the couch to help himself. He was able to focus better now, but his legs were wobbly as he started for the kitchen. He remembered seeing a phone in there.

He called the jail, told Hack what had happened, and asked him to send an ambulance for Marty. "Send Buddy or Ruth, too," he said. "Or both of them. Rolingson's in a BMW." He hung up and went out the back door.

The bright sun dazzled his eyes. There were already little suns dancing in front of them, and the real thing didn't help a bit. He shaded his face with his hand and looked at the garage. The pickup was missing.

Well, that was smart. The pickup was a lot less conspicuous than Rolingson's BMW. Rhodes thought of going back in to call Hack, but he decided to wait and get him by radio. He couldn't afford to waste any more time.

As he shambled toward his own car, he noticed that Rolingson's passing had caused the dust of the gravel road to rise in the still morning air, giving a clear notion of the direction the pickup had taken.

Instead of heading back toward Obert and the main road, Rolingson had gone down the hill toward Appleby's house. That wasn't as dumb as it might seem, either. The county roads were much less traveled than the highways, and although they wound all around over creation, they all came back to a main road sooner or later.

Rhodes got into his car, which with the sun beating down on the top and streaming through the windshield was like getting into a metal box that had been heated in a fire. It didn't do his head any good.

He radioed Hack and told him about the pickup, told him the direction Rolingson was taking.

Hack said that it was no problem and that he would notify Ruth and Buddy. He said that he could get the license number of Graham's pickup with the computer.

"Right," Rhodes said, and then he was off in hot pursuit.

18

▼

HOT PURSUIT WAS THE RIGHT TERM FOR IT, ALL RIGHT, Rhodes thought.

Although he had turned the air conditioner on high and directed all the vents within reach at himself, his entire body was running with sweat. He wasn't sure just how much of that was due to the actual heat and how much to the blow on the head. He hoped it was all the fault of the heat, but he didn't really think it was. He wiped a hand across his slick forehead, wincing when he touched the rapidly growing lump there, and then dried his fingers on his pants leg.

He roared past Appleby's pasture with hardly a glance in the direction of the stolen cattle, which were no longer bunched near the fence. They were getting familiar with the place, beginning to spread out over the pasture. Adkins was luckier than he had any right to be.

The road, like all the country roads, was curvy and tricky. And bumpy, besides. Rhodes had to keep his mind on his driving, not an easy job with a head that felt as if it were expanding and contracting in time to the beat of his heart.

Nevertheless, hick that he was, he had been driving on

roads like that all his life. He knew more or less how his car would respond to the curves and the gravel under the tires, and he had been on that particular road often enough to anticipate the deep ruts, the sandy spots, the places where the gravel was spread too thick or too thin on the curves.

Rolingson, being a city boy, might not know exactly what he was doing. And in one way taking the pickup hadn't been such a smart idea after all. Unlike the BMW, it had rear wheel drive, and when the back end was unloaded, as it was now, it had a tendency to behave differently from the back end of a car.

Rolingson might also not be accustomed to the way the trees grew right up almost to the road, and the tree-whacker had not been used much beyond Appleby's place. The tree branches reached out so close to the road that they almost touched the car doors. Sometimes they *did* touch.

Rhodes hoped all these things would slow Rolingson down enough for Rhodes to catch him.

They did.

Rolingson found out the hard way that driving on the narrow county road wasn't quite the same as sailing along Houston's Gulf Freeway.

Rhodes didn't see it happen, didn't even hear the crash, but he saw the results when the county car topped a little rise in the road.

There was a sharp curve at the bottom of the rise, and Rolingson clearly hadn't been prepared for it. He'd almost made it anyway, but at the last minute the rear tires hadn't taken hold in the loose gravel and the truck had slewed off the road and into the weed-choked drainage ditch.

That in itself might not have stopped Rolingson; with a little driving skill he could have gotten out of the ditch if that had been the only trouble.

But the ditch was still muddy from the Easter spell rains. Rolingson had never been stuck in the mud before, and he had no idea of what to do about it. The one thing he shouldn't have done was to press down on the accelerator as hard as he could and hope that the pickup would pull itself free, but that was what he did.

When Rhodes arrived on the scene, he could hear the high-pitched whine of an engine being revved. He could see the pickup's rear wheels spinning, and he could see the mud that was being flung up behind them.

Rolingson was never going to get the pickup out of the ditch that way, as any hick could have told him.

Rhodes stopped his car and got out. Only then did he realize that he didn't have his pistol. He had no idea where it was, though he thought it was most likely on the couch or on the floor in the front room of Graham's house. He'd had it out of the holster when Marty Wallace crashed into him, and he hadn't thought of it since. He'd been too addled when he left the house to think of it then.

He was still addled, and he was hearing a terrible thrashing noise in his head. He started toward Rolingson, hoping that because of his minor accident Rolingson might be just the least bit confused, too.

If Rolingson was confused, however, he didn't show it. When he saw Rhodes coming, he got out of the pickup and took off down the road in an easy jog.

Rhodes headed after him. Every step he took made him feel as if someone were sitting astride his shoulders and hitting him in the head with a wooden mallet. Marty Wallace's head had been *hard.*

As he followed Rolingson, the thrashing noise seemed to get louder and louder. When Rhodes rounded a curve, Rolingson still well ahead of him and gaining, he saw that the noise wasn't in his head after all.

The tree-whacker was hard at work, and it was coming along the road toward them.

The whacker was built a little like a tractor with a power lawnmower on an arm that could be extended either in front or to the sides. The mower part could be angled as much as ninety degrees to whack off the tree limbs, or it could be lowered to the ground for the brushy cover.

It was making so much noise tearing and breaking the limbs that the county employee driving it had not heard the slamming of car doors when Rhodes and Rolingson got out of their vehicles, and he was paying no attention to the two men running along the road in his direction.

It looked to Rhodes as if the man were wearing a Walkman or a cheap imitation, no doubt with the volume turned up to ten, listening to whatever kind of music he preferred to drown out the noise of the whacking.

Rolingson saw at once the advantages of being in the driver's seat of such a machine if you were being pursued by the county sheriff. He ran alongside the chopper, put his foot on some step that Rhodes could not see, and dragged the surprised driver from the open cab, heaving him roughly out into the middle of the road, where he landed on his back and skidded for a good five feet. Rhodes knew the man's back would be skinned and sore for days.

Rolingson might have been a city boy, but he wasn't without intelligence. He sat in the cab for a few seconds, working the various levers until he found out how to maneuver the mower arm. The next thing Rhodes knew, the chopper was bearing down on him, the mower blade turned toward him and whirling so fast that Rhodes couldn't see it.

Not being able to see it wasn't much comfort however, considering that Rhodes knew it was there. And knew what it could do to a tree.

He could only imagine what it could do to a man, but what he imagined wasn't pretty. It involved arms and legs flying through the air and drops of blood as fine as mist.

He suddenly remembered a neighbor's cat that had a bad habit of getting under cars and climbing up into their engine compartments to sleep. He remembered the day the neighbor had started the car and the cat had been too near the fan blade. It hadn't been a pretty sight.

Rhodes knew that the macho thing to do would be to stand there unmoving, bravely facing certain death by mangling. He also knew that he would be a complete idiot to let Rolingson mow him down. Literally.

He turned and ran.

He was tempted to put a hand on top of his head to keep it from flying off, but he told himself that wasn't really necessary, no matter how imperative it might appear to be. He did it anyway. It seemed to help.

There was another problem. Even if he had been a devoted exerciser and spent an hour or so daily on his Huffy Sunspirit stationary bike, he would have had trouble outrunning the chopper.

As it was, he didn't have a chance.

Not in the road, at any rate. But he didn't think that Rolingson could hit him if he went in the ditch.

Rhodes veered to the right and ran down the side of the ditch, weeds slapping at his pants. When he stepped into the water at the bottom, his left foot sank into mud that covered his shoe almost to the ankle. No wonder Rolingson had gotten the pickup stuck.

Rhodes pulled out his foot, but the shoe stayed in the mud. He didn't have time to feel around for it. Rolingson had angled into the ditch, and the mower blade was spinning crazily not ten feet from Rhodes's unprotected body, which had never felt quite so soft and vulnerable.

There was a hardy-looking elm with low-hanging limbs to Rhodes's right. When he was a kid, he'd spent a lot of time climbing trees like that one, but now he couldn't begin to recall the last time he'd climbed one. Thirty-five or forty years?

Not that it mattered. He grabbed a limb, put his foot—the one with the sock—onto another, and started up.

He could have run into the field, but the barbed-wire fence that surrounded it was rusty and sagging, and the fence posts were rotten. Rolingson would plow right through it and catch him in less than a minute. At least in the tree he might be able to climb higher than the spinning blade could reach.

The whole tree shook when the whacker ripped the lower limbs apart only seconds after Rhodes left them for the upper branches. Bark, leaves, and shredded wood flew around him as he put his arms around the trunk and held on. The noise was awful, and it didn't do a thing to improve Rhodes's headache.

The tree was too thick for Rolingson to destroy with the whacker. He would have needed a chain saw for that. However, he didn't give up. He began raising the arm.

Rhodes didn't think he could go any higher than he already was. The branches wouldn't support him, and falling would be almost as bad as getting whacked.

He went higher anyway.

The mower arm continued to climb.

Tree parts continued to fly.

As a consequence of raising the arm, the vehicle behind it had to come closer and closer to the tree.

Well, Rhodes thought, looking down from his insecure perch, *why not?*

He jumped from the tree and landed on top of the cab with a hollow thud. His shoed foot went out from under him, but the foot with the sock stuck tight. The result was that he fell hard on his right buttock.

The top of his head sailed off into the ditch, or it felt that way. Rhodes put up a hand to check. His head was all in one piece as far as he could tell.

He turned over on his stomach and lowered his head over the side. Rolingson stared back at him with undisguised hatred and swung a boulder-sized fist at his face.

Rhodes jerked back just in time, and Rolingson's fist connected with the edge of the cab top.

The impact bounced Rhodes an inch into the air, and it didn't do his head any good, either.

It did a lot less good to Rolingson's fist, and Rhodes could hear his howl over the furious chopping of the mower blade.

Rhodes looked down again and saw that Rolingson was preoccupied with his hand. Blood was welling out of the skin over the knuckles.

Rhodes didn't have any sympathy to waste on Rolingson. He reached around, grabbed a handful of the T-shirt, and started dragging Rolingson out of the cab. He would probably not have been successful if Rolingson had not been both hurt and surprised. As it was, Rhodes managed to pull Rolingson off the driver's seat and dump him in the mud and weeds of the ditch.

It would have been nice if he could have trusted Rolingson to remain there, but somehow he knew he couldn't. He launched himself off the top of the cab.

Rolingson was lying on his back, and Rhodes landed on top of him, getting a knee into Rolingson's sternum.

Rolingson's face turned completely red as he struggled for breath, and Rhodes thought the fight was over almost as soon as it had begun. He was glad of that.

But he was wrong. Rolingson swung his good left hand up and clouted Rhodes in the face. Rhodes fell off into the muddy water at the bottom of the ditch. He was sure that the top of his head had parted company with him this time.

He didn't have time to investigate. Rolingson was getting to his knees and winding up for another swing.

Rhodes's fingers closed over something in the mud. It was his shoe. It came out of the mud with a sucking sound, water and mud drops flying off it as Rhodes swung it as hard as he could at Rolingson's face.

The sole of the shoe hit Rolingson squarely in the nose. Rhodes felt the nose give way, and there was a gratifying crunching sound.

Rolingson yowled, and his fist went harmlessly by Rhodes's ear. Blood spurted from Rolingson's nose.

Rhodes got up, ready to hit Rolingson again, but he didn't have to. All the fight had gone out of the bigger man, as sometimes happened when it was proved to people that their superior size was not going to be the deciding factor in a fight after all. Rolingson was all right when it came to choking little old ladies or smaller men like Brame, even when hanging men the size of Graham. Getting hurt by someone like Rhodes was a different thing.

Rhodes was dripping with muck and muddy water. Rolingson, who was bleeding, looked even worse.

Over the sound of the tree-whacker, which was still working on the tree, Rhodes heard someone talking to him. It was the county employee, who now had his earphones hanging around his neck.

"You need any help?" the man said.

"Not now," Rhodes said.

"If I'd known there was gonna be mud wrestlin'—"

"Yeah, I know," Rhodes said. "You would have gotten here sooner."

"Right," the man said. "How'd you know that?"

"Never mind," Rhodes said. He nodded toward the whacker. "Can you get that thing shut off? It's giving me a headache."

"Sure." The man walked past Rolingson and climbed into the cab. He turned the key and the engine stopped.

"Thanks," Rhodes said.

He shook water and mud out of his shoe and slipped it on his foot. He felt on his belt, and to his surprise he found that he still had his handcuffs. He walked over to Rolingson and cuffed him. Rolingson's thick wrists were almost too big for the cuffs. Rhodes was very thankful Rolingson hadn't hit him.

Rhodes looked up at the county employee. "You don't see the top of a head anywhere around here, do you?"

"Huh?" The man looked at Rhodes as if he were afraid the sheriff had suddenly gone crazy.

Rhodes put up a hand and touched his hair gently. "Never mind," he said. "There it is."

"Uh, yeah," the man said. "Whatever you say."

Rhodes jerked on the cuffs. "Let's go, Mr. Rolingson," he said. He was glad the county car was already a muddy mess, but it was about to get worse.

"By nodse," Rolingson said. "You brogue by nodse."

"I'm sorry," Rhodes said.

But he wasn't.

Ruth Grady met him as he was going past Appleby's house, and she turned around to follow him back to the college. The EMS vehicle was still at Graham's house when they got there.

"She'll be okay, I think," the young EMT told Rhodes. "Concussion is all. Hell, Sheriff, you look a lot worse than she does."

Rhodes was pretty sure he felt worse, too. "I'll be all right," he said.

"Maybe you better come by the hospital," the young man said. "Let somebody check you out."

"Maybe," Rhodes said.

He told Ruth to follow the ambulance into town and keep a watch on Marty Wallace. "Consider her your prisoner. She's involved in all this up to her neck." Then he asked about fingerprints in the Volvo.

"It had been wiped down, but not very well," she said. "I found a couple."

Rhodes hoped they were Rolingson's, but they wouldn't convict him. Maybe Marty would talk.

"We can search Rolingson's clothes for rope fibers," Ruth said. "If we can find some and get a match with the rope that was used to hang Graham, that might help."

"Good," Rhodes said.

Fiber evidence, fingerprints, a solid motive, and maybe even a witness. Things weren't looking good for Rolingson.

Marty Wallace would likely get a light sentence, Rhodes thought, since she probably hadn't actually killed anyone. And besides, she was a good-looking woman. No matter what anyone said, justice wasn't entirely blind, especially if there were a number of sympathetic men on the jury. But Rolingson was going away for a good long time.

Rhodes felt the top of his head again. He didn't feel sorry for Rolingson at all.

19

▼

"ARE YOU SURE YOU FEEL LIKE GOING ON A PICNIC?" IVY SAID.

"Yep," Rhodes said. He didn't nod for fear that his head might fall off into his lap.

"You don't look like it," Ivy said.

Rhodes had gone home, had a hot shower, washed his muddy clothes, and put on clean ones. He thought he looked pretty good, except for the lump on his forehead, which felt as if it were about the size of a basketball. Then he had gone by the hospital, but not to get checked out. He had talked to Marty Wallace.

"You should have seen the other guy," he told Ivy.

Ivy didn't laugh. "Is it all right for us to go on a picnic in the county car?"

"This isn't just a picnic," Rhodes said. "This is official county business, too."

He had taken the car to the station that the county used and had it cleaned out, though the seat was still a little damp on his side. Ivy's side was fine, since no one had been sitting there. The back seat didn't matter. Any prisoners would have to tough it out.

"Where are we going?" Ivy said.

"Obert," Rhodes said.

* * *

When they got to the college, Rhodes parked in front of the main building. They got out, and Rhodes got the food out of the back seat. It was in a white plastic cooler that had a picture of a big blue bass on the side. Rhodes had made roast beef sandwiches and put them into the cooler along with two Dr Peppers.

"This is a lot better than waiting for you to come home late," Ivy said. "I did sort of want to see *The Searchers,* though."

"We can tape it," Rhodes said. "That's better than staying up. Come on."

"Where are we going?"

"Over there." Rhodes pointed to the rock pile.

"Those things are as big as dinosaurs," Ivy said.

Rhodes thought she was very perceptive. "What are those yellow flowers called?" he said.

"False daisies," Ivy said.

Rhodes wondered if that could be right. When they came to one, he leaned down and looked at it. It looked a lot like a daisy, all right, but he supposed it wasn't one.

Ivy picked one and held it up. "They're smaller than real daisies," she said. She was wearing jeans and an old shirt. Rhodes had called her at work and warned her to change. "What happened to the beautiful woman who was involved in your investigation?"

Rhodes had told her about Marty's being taken to the hospital. "The doctor says that she's going to be fine. Did you go by to see the Appleby women on your way home?"

"Yes. They're both ready to move back to Obert now that it looks certain that Mr. Appleby won't be coming home anytime soon."

"How will they support themselves?" Rhodes said.

"Twyla Faye says she can get a job as a checker in a supermarket. She's done it before. Her mother will sell the cattle that Appleby got legitimately, or the ones that no one has said are stolen, and then she'll try to get a job herself. With her and Twyla Faye both working, they'll do all right. She wants the twins to go back to school, if they get out of jail."

"I think they're going to have to face a few charges," Rhodes said as they reached the rocks.

He had talked to Claude and Clyde earlier, and they still remained silent about what they did or did not know about Simon Graham. Cy Appleby was no longer quite so self-assured, but he still had enough control over the twins to keep them from talking. Rhodes didn't mind. He thought he knew everything Claude and Clyde could have told him.

It was only about four-thirty, and the sun was still in the sky. The rocks had been soaking up the sunlight all day, and they were warm to the touch. Somewhere in the field a quail made its bobwhite call.

"Come on in the shade," Rhodes said, walking into the shelter created by the rocks.

Ivy followed him in. There was no longer any litter there, since Rhodes had carried it away. The ground was smooth, almost as if it had been swept clean.

"Someone's been here before us," Ivy said. "Is this one of your old romantic rendezvous spots?"

Rhodes set down the cooler. "Not a chance. I came here once or twice when I was a teenager, but only to look at the rocks."

Ivy gave him a look.

"I thought they looked like dinosaurs, too," he said.

He opened the cooler and brought out the Dr Peppers. They had been nestled in ice, and the glass bottles were cold and wet. He gave one of them to Ivy. There was a bottle opener tied to a string dangling from the cooler handle, and he opened the bottle he was holding. Then he traded it to Ivy for the other one and opened it.

He took a swallow. "That tastes good," he said.

"What about the sandwiches?"

"Make yourself comfortable," he said. "I'll get them."

Ivy sat down on the hard-packed earth while he got out the sandwiches. Then he joined her on the ground. It had been protected from the Easter spell's rain by the rocks and it felt warm and pleasant.

They unwrapped the sandwiches and ate them. When they were finished, Rhodes took the cooler out in the field and dumped the ice. He brought it back under the rocks and put the sandwich wrappers and bottles inside, then sat down beside Ivy and leaned back against the rocks. He found it very relaxing just to sit there with his eyes closed, not thinking of anything in particular.

"Wake up," Ivy said, giving him a light jab in the ribs.

"I wasn't asleep," Rhodes said. "Just resting my eyes."

"Ha."

"I was," Rhodes said. "I'm awake. Alert. A trained lawman never rests."

Ivy laughed. "What about Rolingson?" she said. "Did he really kill three people just because of a book he couldn't find?"

"I think he did," Rhodes said. "He obviously didn't think we hick lawmen would ever catch him, but at least he tried to make Graham's death look like an accident. By the time he killed the others, he'd decided that we were so dumb he didn't even have to do that."

"What about the book?" Ivy said. "Did it really exist?"

"I think so," Rhodes said.

"And how much did you say it was worth?"

"A quarter of a million, maybe. If it's genuine, that is. If it's not, I don't guess it's worth much of anything, except as a curiosity."

"I don't see why no one could find it," Ivy said.

"It wasn't really a book," Rhodes said. "It was more like a booklet. It could be hidden pretty easily."

"Yes, but still. Those two were searching for days. And

to hear you tell about the way the house looked, they must have done a pretty thorough job."

"Maybe they weren't looking in the right place," Rhodes said.

"Maybe not. It seems a shame that something like that should be lost, though."

"We don't know that it's lost."

"You sound pretty sure of yourself, Dan Rhodes. Do you know where that book is?"

"No," Rhodes said. "I only think I know. I could be wrong."

"And that's why we came to Obert. You're going to find it and prove that Rolingson underestimated you again."

"I'm going to *try* to find it. Hack says there's a big difference between thinking and knowing."

"All right," Ivy said, getting to her feet. "Let's go find it."

"We don't have to go anywhere," Rhodes said.

"What do you mean?"

"I mean I think it's here."

"Right here? In these rocks?"

Rhodes told her about finding the sandwich papers, the aluminum cans, the cigarette filters.

"That doesn't mean anything," Ivy said. "Anyone could have left those here."

"I know. But I think Claude and Clyde did. They strike me as the litterbug type, and this would sure be a convenient place for them to come when they wanted to get away from the house. Boys like private places."

"Did you have one?" she said.

"I did. It was an old deserted house about six blocks from where I lived. Three or four of us used to meet there and talk, swap baseball cards, that kind of thing."

"What about smoking?"

"No smoking. We were afraid we might burn the house down."

"I'd think Claude and Clyde could smoke at home if they wanted to," Ivy said.

Rhodes shrugged. "They probably could, and did. They smoked here, too, though. If it was them."

"Okay, I believe you. But I don't see any book around here."

"I don't think they'd leave it right out in the open," Rhodes said. "We hid things in that house. Comic books. Magazines."

"What kind of magazines?"

"Never mind that," Rhodes said. "What's that in that little crevice over there?" He pointed to a place where two rocks lay together at an angle, a place that was well protected from both sun and rain.

"I don't know," Ivy said, peering at it. "And I'm not going to stick my hand in it and find out, either. It's dark, and there might be snakes in there."

"I've never seen a single rattler in Blacklin County," Rhodes said.

"A snake is a snake," Ivy said. "You can find out what's in the crack if you want to, but I'm not going to stick *my* hand into a place like that."

"Where's your spirit of adventure? There might be a book worth two hundred and fifty thousand dollars in there."

"There might be a brown recluse spider in there, too. Or a stinging scorpion. No thanks."

Rhodes hadn't thought about the spiders. A brown recluse was as bad as a snake, if not worse. Nevertheless, he got up and brushed off the seat of his pants.

"Well, all right, then," he said. "If you don't want to be the hero in this case, I will."

He bent down and put his hand into the crack. He didn't really know what he expected to find there. He had no way of knowing if the litter he had found had really been left there by the twins, and he had no way of knowing that they were the ones who had taken the book.

But they were the ones who had been in the office that first morning, and it was possible that Graham had showed the book to them and bragged about its worth. He might not have told them exactly how much it was worth, but even if he only said that it was worth a lot of money, the twins would have been sorely tempted.

Even if they had taken the book, they might have hidden it somewhere else, like the Haunted House, but Rhodes thought it would be closer to home, somewhere they could get to it easily. This was the best place he could think of.

If he was wrong, well, the worst that could happen was that he would get bitten by a brown recluse and his arm would rot off. Or a rattler would bite him on top of the hand.

His fingers touched slick paper, and he pulled out a handful of magazines. Something clinked in the hole as he pulled the magazines out.

"Is that it?" Ivy said.

"No," Rhodes said. He was holding an old copy of *Penthouse* and two issues of *Playboy.*

"Oh," Ivy said. *"That* kind of magazine."

Rhodes didn't answer. He reached back into the hole and brought out a key ring. There were five or six keys hanging on it.

He hadn't thought he would find that. Claude and Clyde had more to trade than he'd thought. They must have arrived at the main building before Rolingson could search Graham's body. Maybe they had even frightened him away. It looked as if he would have to make a trade with them after all.

He put the keys into his pocket and began flipping through the magazines. The *Tamerlane* was there, slipped in between the *Penthouse* and the first *Playboy.* He pulled it out and held it where Ivy could see it.

It didn't look as old as he had expected. The paper did not have the yellowish tinge that affected most of the old paperback books he had seen in Ballinger's office. Instead, it was brownish', and there were brown spots on it here and there. The edges of the pages were worn, and there were little chips of paper missing from them.

"Doesn't look like much, does it?" he said. "Clyde Ballinger's books have a whole lot better covers."

"And it's worth a quarter of a million dollars?" Ivy said. "Are you sure?"

"That's what I was told. Depending on the condition. I don't know how to describe the condition of things like this, though. It's pretty old."

" 'Poems by a Bostonian,' " Ivy said. "The Bostonian is Mr. Poe, I guess."

"Must be."

"I wonder if the poem's any good," Ivy said. "I don't remember reading that one in high school."

Rhodes didn't either. "El Dorado" and "Annabelle Lee" were the ones he remembered. And a story about some man who got walled up in a wine cellar.

"I guess the twins stole it, then," Ivy said.

"They must have," Rhodes said. "I expect they watched Graham hide it or maybe they guessed where he hid it. I think Marty and Rolingson were frightened away by them after the hanging and that the boys found the keys and searched the office."

He wondered how the twins could have gotten the keys, but then he remembered that there was a ladder in the third-floor room. Claude and Clyde were pretty cold-blooded, no doubt about it.

"What are you going to do with that?" Ivy said, reaching out and touching the *Tamerlane* with a fingertip.

Rhodes thought about it. He could always white out a few words and show it to Mr. Stanley. Probably give the librarian a heart attack. But of course he wouldn't do that.

"I'll keep it in the safe at the jail until we can get rid of it. I'll call to Graham's lawyers. One of them will be here to pick it up tomorrow or the next day."

"Who did he leave the book to, anyway?" Ivy said.

"The University of Texas. Something called the Humanities Research Center."

"What if it's a forgery?"

"It still won't hurt to have it in a safe. I might not be able to find it if it gets stolen again."

"I suppose the picnic's over then, now that the official business is concluded."

"You suppose right. You want to carry the book?"

"No thanks," Ivy said. "I'll carry the cooler." She took the handle and picked it up. "Lead on, Macduff."

"That's something else I remember from high school," Rhodes said. "They were about to have a sword fight, so what Macbeth really said was '*Lay* on, Macduff.' "

Ivy gave him an admiring look. "An intellectual," she said. "I'm impressed."

"Things like that are easy to remember," Rhodes said. "It's phone numbers that give me trouble."

They started back to the car and a bird flew up in front of them.

"You know," Ivy said, watching as the bird circled over their heads, "I always used to call those birds 'feelarks.' I must have been twenty-one years old before I knew better."

Rhodes smiled. He realized that his head didn't hurt anymore. "Me too," he said.